Mathias' Journey

Gordon Beck

Return to Spirit Series

TotalRecall Publications, Inc.
1103 Middlecreek
Friendswood, Texas 77546
281-992-3131 281-482-5390 Fax
www.totalrecallpress.com

ISBN: 978-1-64883-2642
UPC: 6-43977-42642-0

FIRST EDITION
1   2   3   4   5   6   7   8   9   10

I wish to dedicate this writing to my family, friends, and the journeys I have lived.

About the Author

Author, Gordon Beck was born and raised in St. Louis, Missouri. Also raised in part, in the foothills of Missouri, He spent much of his life roaming from state to state.

Gordon is a cab driver by trade, and laborer. He has one other book to his credit: Return to Spirit, A Prayer Warrior's Journey.

He has been inspired to write due to the surroundings of his travels and promptings of family and friends.

About the book

Mathias was born on a cold wintry day in a large midwestern city, with a backdrop of a large river.

Birth was hard on mother and child, due to Mathias having a hernia and other issues. Docie, Mathias' mother, loved him and nurtured him through the illnesses.

Mathias, as a toddler played, played alone most of the time. While his sisters gathered together, making up games to keep them occupied. Docie surely had her hands full raising seven children alone. Docie struggled to keep them fed and clothed on what little she was able to provide through independent work.

As Mathias grew, his mother and sister, Bethany, had to keep watch on him. For he would wander out the door to "go by go", as he put it.

A wandering child from the beginning, started his life of journeys; later to become a prayer warrior.

Join Mathias on his newest journey, to becoming a prayer warrior.

Chapter 1

The day Mathias and Mr. Blackwell drove from the little mountain was hard for the young boy, leaving all he knew.

Tears streamed down Mathias' face as he watched the small mountain slip away and could hear the hawk as it spoke its farewell.

Mr. Blackwell observed Mathias while he drove slowly so the boy could try and grasp the reasons of this journey. Feeling sorrow emanating from Mathias, it moved the man's heart nearly to tears also.

Mathias quietly spoke saying, "Mr. Blackwell, do you know how long I will be at the facility?" The man looked at Mathias thoughtfully for a few seconds, calculating his answer before he spoke. Scratching his head going over conversations with doctors, therapists, and all their staff before answering. He wanted his answer for Mathias to be as precise as could be, saying, "As for time, I am not really sure. But I can tell you this, young man. It should not be a long period of time. Trust me on that." Mathias nodded his head in understanding and quietly said, "Thank you, sir."

Once through the hills, Mathias' hurt turned to wonder as the miles slipped by. While the scenery changed from small hills to flat and flying by at a rate, as if flying in another dreamscape, nearly confusing by its mere motion. The wind flowing through the partially opened window brought a refreshing breath to Mathias due to the scent of the pine trees they were passing huddled to the woodside, like tall soldiers carrying important messages.

Mr. Blackwell steered the car onto interstate 55, heading north toward a large city where Mathias was born. Speaking to Mathias, "We will be in the city where you were born in approximately one and a half hours. It will then take us about thirty or so minutes to reach the facility your testing will be in. Are you comfortable? Mathias answered Mr. Blackwell, he was just fine now.

CHAPTER 11

Mathias drifted in and out of sleep by the car's motion, along with the "click, click, click" of its tires. Sleep brought images of places far away, drifting like clouds. Yet not clear enough to grasp the images of places far away. One after another, they floated. Mathias couldn't reach them as he traveled the dreamscapes. Suddenly, his guardian appeared before him speaking words of encouragement to soothe the days' mind. Knowing he was dreaming yet understanding the words of his guardian, brought comfort through clarity.

A jolt jarred Mathias awake. Looking at Mr. Blackwell with a look of concern on the man's face, Mathias asked him, "What is it, Mr. Blackwell?" The man spoke saying, "Mathias, you were mumbling and speaking in what sounded a foreign language to me. Were you dreaming?" Mathias could only nod his head in a yes gesture.

The miles clicked on and seemed to never end. All the traffic signs, and all the clatter filled Mathias' mind. Mr. Blackwell spoke of the facility saying, "We will be arriving at the facility momentarily where your testing will be, Mathias. This trip now is almost over. We will get you signed in, the staff will show us around, and where you will be housed. Okay?" Once again, Mathias nodded a yes.

Chapter III

A forlorn feeling had settled on Mathias. Knowing not what to expect, he delved deeper into himself. Mr. Blackwell kept speaking and Mathias really wasn't listening. Instead, he drifted into a half sleep. Mathias was brought out of his half-sleep by the car turning into a long asphalt driveway that traveled into a circle at the end of it.

Mr. Blackwell touched the boy on his left shoulder saying, "Mathias we are here at the facility we have spoken of. Come let us enter into this journey." Mathias liked how the man presented to him what would surely prove to be exactly that, a journey.

As Mathias & Mr. Blackwell exited the vehicle, they were met by a friendly, smiling lady and a kindly middle-aged man both dressed casually and not in clinical attire.

"Hello" was the greeting. Holding out their hands in a welcoming gesture, the woman spoke introducing the two of them, saying, "I am Grace Strong. This is Don Hammerman. We are the coordinators here at Heilemann Facilities. We direct the staff at the behest of our doctors." While the woman spoke, Mathias' attention was drawn to a figure of a man partially hidden by a heavy dark blue drapery. Mathias felt a negative vibration from his instincts.

Ms. Strong looked at the figure by the drapery with a slight grin. She told Mathias, "That man is Dr. Granger. He is our head spiritual director. He is harmless, Mathias. He is just inquisitive." Mathias looked away yet thinking, *'he is more than meets the eye, ma'am.'*

With that, the four of them began walking up the few wide steps onto a stone and concrete type porch foreign to Mathias. Once inside, a large room opened up to what appeared to be a doctor's large office setting. Suddenly, thunder roared which startled the adults. Yet not Mathias, he we was not affected by the loudness. He looked at the three adults with a sheepish grin and said, "thunder beings".

Mathias watched from his peripheral vision, the figure of Mr. Granger lurking in the shadow, still somewhat hidden by the heavy drapery; perhaps feeling no one noticed his presence. Momentarily, Mathias waved his right hand as to dismiss the image of the man. Suddenly the man slipped away in a shadowy manner. Mathias could only giggle quietly at the man's antics. All the while, the three adults looked to one another in a bemused silence.

Chapter IV

Ms. Strong suggested the four of them tour the facility and the grounds so Mathias could get familiar with his surroundings. Walking through the tiled hallways, there were pictures of mountains, valleys along with beautiful flowers & plants of different origins, paintings by semi-famous artists, also some prints; all placed to coordinate with the purpose of a peaceful environment. Mathias took in his memory each picture and the feeling it brought to him. There were rooms fashioned for bedrooms, living rooms, and rooms for entertainment with board games, as well as other types of games. Mathias looked with little interest, catching a glance of Mr. Granger as they glimpsed into each room. He pondered on the fact of the man lurking as he pretended not to see him.

Ms. Strong noticing Mathias' uninterested aire, she halted the tour and turned to Mathias saying, "Mathias, are you with us?" Mathias shrugged his shoulders as though it made no difference to him. Ms. Strong looked thoughtful for a minute, then stated, "I bet you want to see the grounds." Mathias smiled widely, showing his enthusiasm.

Ms. Strong led the way to a rear door with Mr. Granger slipping from doorway to doorway as a scepter floating, obviously curious. Stepping into the outdoors for Mathias was as walking into a different zone; hearing the leaves rustle showing their attractiveness. The main grounds held trees spaced apart to add a look of grassy areas well-manicured to delight the senses. Pine, oak, a few apple, peach & evergreen, and other spices made up the scenery. At the edge of the lawn area was also honey suckle so the hummingbirds had adequate food for their little bodies' nourishment.

A calmness always came over Mathias when he encountered nature and its beauty. His senses basked in the feel and smell to his delight. There came a call of the hawk to their ears. Mathias watched skyward to find the source of the winged raptor. Hawk circling high above them in a left direction. Ms. Strong looked toward Mathias and asked, "What bird is that Mathias?" The boy looked at her and replied, "It is Hawk flying in a left direction, in the way of woman." Ms. Strong appeared interested so Mathias helped her to understand that Hawk was a messenger showing that a woman was going to call about him. Hawk flew in the direction where Mathias lived. Mathias then told Ms. Strong his aunt Anias would be calling shortly to inquire of his travel which brought him and Mr. Blackwell to their destination safely. Strange looks all around from the adults spoke of them not understanding what the boy was saying.

The outside tour lasted a good half hour, going in and out of the trees. Peering through branches at them were squirrels, along with woodpeckers, robins, and cardinals, male, female, and the young offspring of the animals. Then it was time to return to the main building. For dinner time was approaching.

Chapter V

Upon arriving at the building door, Mr. Strong was notified by a staff member that Mathias' Aunt Anias had made a phone call asking about Mathias and Mr. Blackwell's safe arrival. With that, the adults looked at Mathias in a wondering way; thinking, *'how did he know?'* Mathias only looked at each one smiling in a way that said, *'You didn't know, did you?'*

Dinner time awaited Mathias and all that occupied the facility, along with the staff. Stuffed cabbage was the main fare, including macaroni casserole, sweet cornbread, pinto beans, and large pitchers of sweet and unsweet tea. To finish the fare was banana pudding freshly made and ice cream.

Mathias met other children and adults gifted in different areas, which made for interesting conversation. Chatter filled the dining hall. He made an effort to join in, which wasn't difficult, considering the topics of talk.

After dinner, everyone disbursed to their perspective places. Ms. Strong along with Mr. Hammerman, Mr. Blackwell, and Mathias strolled through the dining hall, then out into the hallway. They were going to show Mathias where he would be sleeping, spending part of his time there. Where he could rest his mind. At this time, a calming wave of music filled the hallways as each person listened tentatively, bringing a sense of peace and wellbeing. The four made their way along a large hallway with signs above doorways designating the rooms' purpose. This hallway was the living quarters for clients' comfort. Mathias peered into each room while passing, wondering what the evening would bring.

Ms. Strong could see Mathia's apprehension concerning his plight, her saying, "Mathias, all will be fine. You will be able to relax here. You'll have no chores to occupy your time here." They stopped before a door which, when Mathias looked up at the top, was a plaque with his name on it. Surprised by the unexpected pleasure of his name plaque, his eyes shone brightly, and he sighed heavily with a feeling of relief and knowing surely, he was in a safe environment.

Mr. Blackwell informed Ms. Strong, Mr. Hammerman, and Mathias he would be leaving them within a few minutes, for his duties awaited him. Looking at Mathias, Mr. Blackwell stated, "Sorry son, my time here has expired. I must return and fill out a report saying our journey here went as planned and you are at the facility, I was expected to bring you to." Mathias asked him, "Will you be coming back for me soon?" The man said he would be the one to come for Mathias when the staff had completed their tests that was required. With that, Mr. Blackwell turned to leave with a wave goodbye. He walked down the hallway, turning around a few feet away. He waived his right hand in a farewell gesture toward Mathias. In turn, Mathias did likewise with a sad smile.

Standing in the doorway to Mathias' room, the three observed something strange carved into the wood frame. Looking closer, Mr. Hammerman described what was visible to the eyes. Slowly tracing the shape of a feather, with a circle with a line through it below the feather. Looking closely, Ms. Strong and Mathias both sighed; them looking at one another. Mr. Hammerman ask the woman, "What do you make of this, Ms. Strong?" The woman replied, "I'm not sure. This wasn't here before, that we know of." All the while, Mathias stood silent; yet knowing the meaning, keeping it to himself. At that moment the trio could hear a wolf howl, the sound coming from a distance. During that few minutes, Mr. Granger could be seen peeking around a corner of the hallway, then swiftly retreating.

Time had passed since Mathias and Mr. Blackwell arrived. Dinner was done. A tour of the grounds and the facility was looked over. Night was calling with whispers of the wind within the trees. An old owl spoke softly of life within the facility walls.

Ms. Strong walked into the bedroom, which was to be Mathias' while he would be a visitor there. Also, Mr. Hammerman and Mathias strolled into the room. Quietly, as they took at the bed, nightstand with a reading lamp, a portable closet made of metal with white-thick cotton covering it. The front was open to reveal a long rod for hanging clothes and side pockets for shoes and other items.

While the trio was talking inside the room that was Mathias' bedroom, Ms. Strong walked to the window and started raising the blind that covered it. While raising the blind, she was talking, looking over her right shoulder at Mr. Hammerman and Mathias. She turned back to the window. Suddenly, she let go of the pull string holding the blind. She jumped back a few feet, letting out a gasp, pointing to the window, speechless, turning pale, then stammering something unintelligible facing toward the window, then collapsed where she stood. Mr. Hammerman rushed forward just in time to catch her (to keep her from falling onto the hard flooring). Meanwhile, Mathias smiling, stood quietly watching.

Chapter VI

Night had fallen. Ms. Strong had awakened from her collapse and bid Mathias a restful night, instructing the boy to be aware of the window. With that, her and Mr. Hammerman exited the bedroom leaving Mathias to himself.

Footsteps in the hallway brought Mathias to the doorway. Peering left and right along the hallway, Mathias made out the figure of Mr. Granger walking slowly toward the outside door then turned right into another room. *'Strange'*, Mathias thought. *'Mr. Granger sure is a wistful being, trapsing the hallway like a ghost, never speaking or appearing before anyone.'* With that, Matias said to himself, "Time for sleep". Laying in bed, visions overtook Mathias' thoughts:

Seeing in the night, as an owl in flight,

Storms thunderous, lightening flash,

Great wonder, chaos and plunder.

Awakening suddenly, there in the doorway stood Mr. Granger, seemingly lost in thought. Mathias quickly moved to exit the bed. Just as he looked again, Mr. Granger was no longer there. Rubbing sleep from his eyes, Mathias slowly made his way to the doorway. Once again, looking in both directions for the allusive man that was just standing there. He was nowhere to be seen.

Mathias made his way into the hallway; walking in the direction of the outside door, shuffling along at a snail's pace, wanting to see what may lay ahead. Finally, he came to the exit. Turning the doorknob, a low-pitched sound pierced the silent hallway causing Mathias to jump in surprise. Mathias turned as a voice called to him, "Young man, no one is allowed to leave the facility after lights out. There are policies put in place to assure that."

With Heavy footsteps, a rather large man seemed to glide to where Mathias stood. Speaking, Mathias stated, "I was only wanting to see where Mr. Granger had gone to." The large man laughed quietly by saying, "You'll not find Mr. Granger. For he is not here." The large man said to Mathias, "I am George, the watchman here at Heilemann. I am the security head. So, if you would please stay within this hallway at night. No one is to exit the building without prior permission.

Mathias closed his eyes for a moment. When he opened them, the man was no longer standing there, but he made his way halfway down the hallway chuckling to himself. *What a mystery* thought Mathias. He hadn't even heard Mr. George walk away. Mathias stood there for at least a full minute, then shuffled his way back into his assigned room wondering what else will happen. A smile crossed his face, for he loved mystery. Wondering what Mr. George meant, Mathias pondered that too.

Back in the assigned room, the boy lay back in the bed drifting while thinking, *What am I missing?* Sleep overtook him. The dreamscape surrounded Mathias, seeing twisters of dust devils swirling, picking up small objects once laying in a heap. Suddenly, appearing his guardian standing next to the dust devil closest to Mathias. Speaking urgently, telling Mathias, "You are entering a path of destruction in your life. It shall be for many years, young warrior. This shows the turbulence surrounding your path. I will be there for you at all times. Dream on."

Mathias awoke panting and sweating. Light showed down the hallway from the outside. Morning had come too quickly for the young boy. Sitting up, the boy rubbed his eyes, groggy from the heavy sleep. Sunlight shone on the hallway floor reminding Mathias of where he was (at Heilemann facility). His mind taking in what was going to be a long day of testing and where it would begin. Breakfast would be first on the day's agenda.

CHAPTER VII

With breakfast finished, there was a bustle in the hallways at Heilemann. Mathias thinking this is like the schools he had attended. *The same loud talking and the shuffling of many feet, 'blah, blah, blah',* he thought.

Ms. Strong corralled Mathias by taking his arm in hers and directed him into another hallway speaking with a lighthearted voice, saying, "Come along, Mathias. Let us see what the list of tests has in store for us." Mathias could only walk along, being that he was guided by his left arm and feeling out of control of his footsteps. Mathias asked, "Where is Mr. Granger?" Ms. Strong assured him that Mathias wouldn't see Mr. Granger today.

Mathias and Ms. Strong entered into a room with machines that looked as though they belonged in a hospital setting. Immediately, they were met by a young female tech. Reaching the two, she extended her right hand to Mathias saying, "I am Sheila Watson. I am the tech here that will be performing x-rays and brain waive tests to determine there is no damage and monitor the electrical waves coming from your brain to assure everything works in accordance with what we know scientifically. Okay, Mathias?" Mathias responded with a nod, while taking in everything around him. Mathias asked Ms. Strong, "Will you be here with me, Ma'am?" The lady answered, "Yes, Mathias, if you will be more comfortable. Yet Sheila here is a kindly person and would help make you feel safe." With a shrug, Mathias let Ms. Strong know that he wanted her there with him.

Mrs. Watson reached once again for Mathias' right hand saying, "Come, Mathias. Let us begin by doing x-rays of your head in six different positions so we can determine there is no damage. And see what, if any, abnormalities may be there. Then, we can continue with the EEG."

After the x-rays, Mrs. Watson let Mathias know it would take a few days for the radiologist to examine them and would write a report on his findings." Next comes the test of Mathias' signals of his young brain. Mathias asked Mrs. Watson what the test was called she would be performing. Mrs. Watson stated, "The test is what is called an electroencephalogram that is the clinical term." She also said that Mathias' REM movement was very rapid, faster than any she had ever observed.

Due to the time involved conducting the second test they just performed, it was lunch time. So, the three agreed to time out, to eat, so they could continue with another test which would be conducted by another tech. Leaving the test room, there came a loud scream echoing through the halls which unnerved Ms. Strong. Mrs. Watson jumped out of fright. She observed Mathias, seemingly unmoved by the suddenness of the loud noise.

Ms. Strong led the trio toward the commotion into another hallway where the scream originated. Through a doorway, they observed several people standing in a semi-circle with a female laying limp on the floor, head bleeding, and what appeared to be urine under her lower half. Ms. Strong stuttering slightly, ask the closest person to the young lady, "What happened to this girl?"

Turning to face Ms. Strong, the young man stated, "The girl had fainted out of fright!" And he wasn't really sure why, being she was in the room alone. "So, we came running to see what the scream was about and found her lying on the floor."

Hearing footsteps behind them (those in the room where the girl had fainted), they turned to see Mr. Hammerman entering the room to inquire of the commotion. Ms. Strong, speaking, said to Mr. Hammerman, "It appears this young lady has fainted, causing injury to her head." Seeing the girl moving about, Mr. Hammerman made his way to her. Pointing toward the doorway, he said to those standing over the girl, "Whomever that are not staff, would you please exit the room and go back to your assigned place. Or go to the dining hall for lunch, so we can figure out what has occurred here. Thank you."

While everyone, except the staff, made their way toward the dining hall. Mathias walked toward the hallway that led to the rear exit. Reaching that hallway, he met another security man approaching him. Mathias asked would he be able to gain permission to walk the grounds so he could breathe some fresh air.

Upon hearing Mathias' request, the man radioed his supervisor on duty. Request was granted. So, the man and Mathias made their way toward the exit. Arriving there, the man said to Mathias, "You will be able to have an hour on the grounds as my supervisor had stated. And please, stay within eyesight. With this, Mathias agreed, shaking his head yes and exited the building.

Feeling the fresh air, Mathias breathed heavily to take in the energies of nature. Looking to the far edge of the lawn, Mathias could make out an object moving slowly toward him. Walking forward at a slow pace with an eerie feeling, stopping abruptly, awaiting what was coming to him. Mathias could finally make out the dark figure pointing at him. The shape was that of a man. The figure stopped approximately 10 feet from him.

Mathias heard the grating voice saying, "You will feel and see the darkness soon in your life. Prepare your heart & mind." Wide eyed, Mathias could see a figure standing directly behind the dark shape; his guardian saying something to the dark figure. Suddenly, the dark figure disappeared, leaving Mathias with a question in his mind of what it could mean. His guardian made his way to Mathias. Close enough, he could hear him clearly saying, "Young man, the dark figure is a warning for you to heed. Watch your footsteps in this path. Try to stay away from those who will lead you to a destructive way of life, with many bad decisions. Beware of the altering chemicals you will be exposed to. Listen and remember my words, young warrior."

As quickly as the two entities appeared, they were gone as of a mist in front of Mathias' eyes. Instinctively, Mathias knew the dark figure was of what is known as, shadow people; the entities of a dark nature which walks the earth.

Mathias' guardian had sent the shadow-being away with a few words; leaving Mathias standing quietly appraising the situation at hand. Suddenly, hearing a voice behind him, Mathias turned to find Mr. Hammerman beaconing him to return to the facility's rear entrance. Looking from where he stood, Mathias realized he was a goodly length from the building entrance. He thought, *'I don't remember walking this far from the doorway?'* Mathias quickly walked across the yard to where Mr. Hammerman awaited him.

Chapter VIII

Evening at Heilemann was a fiasco, beings the fact of the young lady that had the unfortunate fall from fright. They were questioning her, yet not being pushy.

Walking inside, Mr. Hammerman asked Mathias if he had lunch. Mathias answered, "No." So, him and Mr. Hammerman made their way to the lunch area, where other clients were still partaking and conversing. Everyone stopped and watched the two enter the doorway. Mr. Hammerman informed Mathias he would be picking up his lunch and retreating to where the staff gathered to eat together. With that said, they parted ways.

After eating, the entire group dispersed to their prospective places to await decisions on their schedules for the evening. Mathias was called to the front office by the loudspeaker, stating he has a call from home. With that, Mathias cringed; feeling a need to run out onto the grounds to avoid the call. For he knew it was Aunt Anias and he really didn't want to talk to her.

Ms. Strong met Mathias in the hallway, which was the front office. She noticed Mathias' demeanor. She spoke saying, "Mathias. Why look so gloomy?" In turn, Mathias looked away and shrugged his shoulders, as if to say what he was feeling he would keep to himself.

Standing in the office with a blank stare, while listening to the voice on the other end, saying in his head, *'I'll be glad when this call is over.'* Finally, his aunt asked him if he was doing okay so far. Mathias quietly said, "It's fine." She stated the Department of Family Services had called her, and they were going to be doing a home visit due to someone from the school reporting something out of place in the home. So, she asked him if he had spoke to anyone concerning home-life. Mathias simply stated, "No", he hadn't. His aunt then said she had to end their call and should he want, he could call any time. With that, they both hung up.

Ms. Strong informed Mathias, her nor anyone else would be engaging in any clinicals this evening due to investigating the falling of the young lady. She also asked Mathias if he would want to share of the phone call from his aunt, for he seemed troubled. Looking at Ms. Strong, Mathias asked if they could talk elsewhere privately. For what he has to share, he did not want to speak of it here. Turning to the intake worker, Ms. Strong asked her to make the announcement that there would be no clinicals scheduled for this evening. All testing sessions will resume the next day.

Making their way to a more private room, Mathias' mind wandered as he stumbled (Ms. Strong, lifting him by his right arm). She asked him, "Mathias, what is wrong?" Mathias never answered, yet made his way into an empty room, which happened to be a conference room.

Walking to a long table and chairs, Mathias sat at the first chair available while Ms. Strong sat next to him and waited for him to speak. After a few minutes of silence, Mathias started telling Ms. Strong of the phone call he received from his aunt. She informed him that the Department of Family Services had called his aunt. And the department worker would be entering their home to talk with Anias and his sisters on the concerns the department has, concerning a phone call they received and would not go into details. Other than they would address Mathias within a week when they arrive. Ms. Strong sat intensely listening, so Mathias could feel comfortable and know she cared about him and his feelings.

Seeing Mathias's eyes become glassy before he shifted his chair to where he faced away from Ms. Strong (not wanting her to see his tears now streaming down his face; the emotions taking over him.) Quietly sobbing, knowing another person was present, not wanting Ms. Strong to see his face. For Mathias, his tears were private. Finding out years later, his mother was the same way about crying around others. He also knew it was not a weakness, yet a strength to always remember. Ms. Strong finally spoke, saying to Mathias, "Do you want or need to go home, Mathias?" He shrugged his shoulders then raised his right hand in a gesture to give him a few minutes. With that, she patted his left shoulder in a manner that she hoped would comfort him.

After wiping his face with both hands, Mathias turned himself and his chair to face the woman (Ms. Strong) with a faint smile. He looked at her, then hung his head to avoid any eye contact so he could focus on what was going through his mind. Ms. Strong struck up the conversation with asking, "Mathias, do you want to talk about this?" With that statement, Mathias peered up at Ms. Strong and said, "I don't know where to start. There has been things I'm not sure of, if I should speak about with others."

Ms. Strong informed Mathias that there was a therapist he could talk with. Of course, that would be his choice, anytime he would want while he was at Heilemann. Mathias half smiled and said he would think on it. With that, Ms. Strong asked him; was he ready to leave the conference room. Suddenly, Mr. Hammerman stepped into the room. Walking up to the table, stating to Ms. Strong, he had been searching for the two of them. Ms. Strong told him they had been discussing the call Mathias had received and that they were ready to leave the conference room. Mr. Hammerman asked; was there anything he could do. Both Mathias and Ms. Strong shook their heads in a no gesture. So, Mr. Hammerman said, "Okay then." The three of them exited the room.

CHAPTER IX

Evening fell upon the facility. Dinner had been had by all of the residents and staff, leaving everyone full and satisfied body and mind wise. Being there would be no clinicals this evening, everyone took advantage fully and busied themselves with games, letter writings, calls to home, and milling around the halls, just enjoying their day. Meanwhile, Mathias had retired to his room to rest his mind after hearing of the news at home.

While he rested, he fell into a sleep; seeing movements that took him to his home. He witnessed his Aunt Anias and her husband questioning his oldest sister, Bethany, of why or what she knew of the phone call to the family service's staff. Bethany standing in front of them, slightly shaking her head. With little Alamena looking scared and confused by the loud voices coming from the two adults: seeing Anias slap Bethany. Mathias awakened abruptly, sweating, looking around, wondering of what he saw in dream time. Slowly making his way to his feet, Mathias made his way to the doorway and into the hallway. He started walking the hallway in stocking feet so as to not disturb others.

Mathias walked to the left through the hall. Coming to another hallway, he could make out low noises coming from the conference room he had been in earlier. Silently shuffling to the closed door, he peered inside. His vision was met by Ms. Strong and Mr. Hammerman kissing passionately (apparently unaware of anyone observing them). Mathias slowly and quietly opened the door. It was louder than he expected so as to alert the two staff members. Ms. Strong quickly turned away from Mr.

Hammerman; breathlessly exclaiming to Mathias, "Young man, why are you spying on us here?" Just as quickly, Mathias jolted away from apparently another dream. Yet Mathias understood the dreams he has had, will appear within a short period. Or will materialize approximately a year later the one's he remembers. With that thought, Mathias lay back and let his body and mind fall back into a deep sleep feeling exhausted.

Day break came with a flurry of activity. Noisy voices awakened Mathias from his restful sleep. Peering into his room, Mr. Hammerman spoke to Mathias, saying, "Wake up, Sleepy head. The day is starting, and breakfast is on in the dining room. Hurry along so there is plenty to fill you. And by the way, another client observed you slowly walking down the hallway looking as if you were sleeping. You turned back to your room, slipped inside, and did not come back out. The person supposed you went back to bed." Mathias could only stare at Mr. Hammerman while waiting to get dressed. Mr. Hammerman waved a farewell to Mathias and had a small grin on his face and winked at the boy. Mathias knew what he had saw. And now realized he walked in his sleep yet was able to see through the sleep haze.

Mathias dressed. Then made his way to join the others for breakfast. While passing the next hallway, a young lady stopped to inform him he would be speaking with a spiritual counselor when he finished his breakfast. Mathias asked if it were to be Mr. Granger. The young lady looked funny at Mathias. Then, said, "No Mathias. I really don't think Mr. Granger will be seeing you. It will be Mrs. Hopson." Mathias could only look at the woman. Then shook his head in a knowing gesture. Breakfast consisted of different breakfast meats, potatoes fixed in different ways, eggs fried and scrambled, berries, nuts, and a variety of muffins, cold cereal, with other fixings and of course, milk and tea.

Eating breakfast for Mathias was certainly a treat; partaking a small bit in most of what was available. Listening to the chatter unsettled Mathias a bit. He wished he had a way to block out the voices, yet he would deal with it all. For it wouldn't be long before he exited the room, and the noise. He could only look around him and shake his head slightly, so as not to be noticed. While eating, there appeared before him, his guardian speaking of what was to occur at his home today. His guardian assured him he would be fine and would remain at Heilemann until the staff was finished with their tests. "Worry not." said his guardian, "You are safe here. Try and keep yourself in control of your senses. Answer not of what you do not understand." With the talk done, his guardian vanished.

After eating, the same young lady approached Mathias asking him if he was ready to follow her to see Mrs. Hopson. Mathias answered he was and started walking with her. Abruptly Mathias stopped walking. The young lady stopped also and asked Mathias, "Is there something wrong?" Answering her, he simply asked, "What is your name, ma'am?" The young lady smiled saying, "I am Jenny Most. I am a staff member here. I am the one whom was sent to escort the people here to see the head clinical personnel. Okay?" Mathias nodded that he understood. Ms. Jenny Most asked him, "You don't speak much, do you Mathias?" The boy simply shook his head no and quickly said, "No". The two made their way through the hallways coming to an office. The door plaque read 'Mrs. Hopson, Head Spiritual Director'. Looking back down the hall, Mathias could see Mr. Granger peering at them from a shadow, waving at him. Mathias, in kind, returned the wave. Ms. Jenny Most noticed him waving with a wary grin. She shuffled Mathias into the office introducing him to Mrs. Hopson. Speaking to Mrs. Hopson, Ms.

Most stated, "Ma'am, this is Mathias. He is a very bright young man yet is troubled by his spiritual side."

Mathias stood quietly, waiting for Mrs. Hopson and Ms. Most to finish conversing (looking into the hallway and seeing residents making their way to their scheduled meetings with clinicians).   While looking, Mathias could see Mr. Granger walking slowly as though there was no hurry. Turning to the two women, Mathias asked, "Why doesn't Mr. Granger come to speak to me? He seems very evasive." With the question, both women at once turned to Mathias and asked him if he saw Mr. Granger. Mathias assured them he had seen Mr. Granger a few times and he was just walking down the hallway, away from the room they were in. Astonished looks passed between the two women. With a wary smile, Mrs. Hopson answered Mathias with a sketchy answer (leaving the subject to be spoke of at another time).

Ms. Most excused herself, leaving Mathias and Mrs. Hopson to their scheduled meeting; so, Mrs. Hopson could talk with Mathias and run through tests to determine how the boy's belief system may affect him. First, Mrs. Hopson asked Mathias about his religious training at home. With that question, Mathias asked, "What is that?" (For he knew nothing of religious training.) The woman then asked if Mathias and his siblings had ever attended church. Mathias could only shrug his shoulders. Mrs. Hopson then asked, had they ever been to a tent church revival. Mathias answered, yes. They had a few times. The woman then asked if he understood the workings of church revivals.   Mathias looked sheepishly at Mrs. Hopson, not answering her. To assure Mathias, what he may say to her (Mrs. Hopson), would be kept between them. Mrs. Hopson then said, "Mathias, what happened at these revivals?" Mathias once again looked sheepishly, hesitating. Then said, "The preacher was loud, dancing around, talking of hell, & brimstone for sinners." "Is that all, Mathias", asked Mrs. Hopson. Looking down at his feet, Mathias answered quietly, "No". Mathias finally answered again, "They caught my Aunt Anias and the preacher behind the tent having sex. The elders of the church caught them. They told the preacher to leave and not return. Aunt Anias, they walked her into the tent and announced her a 'bible toting harlot'. Then walked us to the entrance and told her never to return. The preacher's wife ran out the front and disappeared through the maze of cars." (At this time, Mathias was at the age of 13 years when he was at Heilemann for testing.)

Mrs. Hopson stood looking at Mathias; wondering how that revelation would affect him later in the years. Next, she talked with him about his dreams. Were they clear most of the time or clouded? Mathias answered, "Both." Mrs. Hopson went on to ask him if he believed in his dreams. Mathias answered "yes", the ones he remembers, "They are very clear." Mrs. Hopson asked him of the things he sees in his waking time; if they too are clear or thought. Mathias said, "clear and sometimes thought," that comes to him like a vision, yet not seeing it is just thought. Mrs. Hopson asked Mathias, "Do you read the bible?" Mathias shook his head no. "Do you believe there is a God, Mathias", the woman asked. His answer was, "Yes". She asked, "How do you know there is a God, Mathias?" He simply said, "I just know".

Mrs. Hopson was writing while her and Mathias spoke. Taking notes of their conversation, the woman asked Mathias, "Do you lie, Mathias?" The boy sat upright and stated, "No. We get a beating if we lie and slapped even backwards in our chair at the dinner table. Then we have to leave the table and are sent to bed to not finish eating." The shock on Mrs. Hopson's face grew as Mathias told of what happens when lying. Mrs. Hopson (with hands shaking) stopped writing. Then Mathias told her of the time the man, Baxter, had threatened the boys with a hot poker; making them bend over their couch and said he would burn them if one of them didn't tell the truth about something that happened. All were crying, begging not to be burned. The one brother admitted to the little infraction that was done. And him sending all to bed, except the one whom admitted the wrong.

Taken aback by what Mathias had divulged, Mrs. Hopson told Mathias, "I believe we are finished for now, Mathias". Mathias nodded his head and Mrs. Hopson called for Ms. Most to escort Mathias to the dining room. For surely it was time to end this session (Mrs. Hopson feeling Mathias was fabricating his story).

Chapter X

Mathias ate alone in silence, barely looking at anyone in the lunchroom. Going through his memory, Mathias searched for any happy times; trying to seek even one. Try as he may, the boy had no memory of any laughter. Surely there were times. But the boy came short of any. Walking through the halls of his mind, Mathias could see visions of a few happenings. One was of his brother Dalton being burned by a big red hot King stove, on his rear end. It seems him and another sibling, was pushing and shoving in a playful manner. Apparently, Dalton was pushed into the red-hot stove, receiving a large burn on one side of his rearend. Dalton screamed in pain. One of the adults grabbed him and took him into another room. And they removed his pants to expose the large burn. Mathias was standing quietly (watching while his siblings stood with fear on their faces), waiting to see if any one of them would be whipped for their transgression of scuffling in the barn (where they lived at the time). Dalton had second degree burns from the stove. They had placed something on the burn. Then he was taken to Baxter's sister's home, where he stayed for quite some time so he could heal. After that, Mathias had no memory for a time. All was blank at that moment.

Mathias ate slowly, not wanting to leave the dining hall just yet. A young girl (approximately the same age as Mathias) walked to the table and introduced herself as Patty. She waited for Mathias to respond. Finally speaking (saying shyly), "I am Mathias." The girl asked if it was okay if she could sit with him. He nodded yes without looking at her. For Mathias had never, not once, spoke with any girls besides his sisters.

Patty started chattering about school and why she was at Heilemann. She asked Mathias why he was there. He simply stated, to be tested and answer questions of his behaviors. The girl asked him if had been misbehaving at home. Mathias stated he had not. They wondered why he sees and hears things others do not see or hear. Patty looked seriously at Mathias and realized that she could relate to what he said. She told Mathias, "I hear people speaking to me, that are looking at me and their mouth would not be moving. Do you experience that too, Mathias?" Mathias shook his head in a yes gesture, yet not speaking.

Talking to this girl (Patty) seemed so easy. It made Mathias feel comfortable. Where with others, he didn't converse. He would only shake his head or shrug his shoulders. The girl had brought her tray of food with her. She kept talking, hardly drawing a breath. Which was fine with Mathias. For he was not a conversationist. She told him her age and she had 5 siblings at home. Yet she was the only one that her family knew of, that had these experiences. Finally, Patty asked Mathias if he had seen Mr. Granger lurking around in the hallways yet could never approach him.

She also said when she would ask of him (Mr. Granger), the staff would tell her not to be concerned of him. "Strange." she said.

The loudspeaker came on and informed everyone that this evening would be movie night. Patty asked Mathias if he would go and share movie night with her. Shyly Mathias accepted saying, "yes", he would. Finishing their dinner at the same time, Patty winked at Mathias and said, "I'll see you at 7:00 this evening in the movie room. He gave a silly grin and said, "Okay". Patty sauntered off happily talking to herself while Mathias watched. And thinking, *she is a friendly soul*.

Mathias had time as did others, before movie time. He wandered to the rear entrance of the building. This time, no one came to check to see of why he was there. Skipping along the hallway toward Mathias was Patty just chattering away at no one in particular. Smiling a large smile, she reached Mathias. Placing her hand on his, she said, "They don't want us outside alone. There are large predators on the grounds. Which no one has attempted to trap and take them to where they can be released unharmed. But, you and I are able to be amongst them. Where others cannot be, due to fear on their part."

The young girl suggested to Mathias that the two of them could go to Mathias' room and talk, since they had a few hours before they were to head to the movie room. Mathias studied Patty for a brief moment and said, "Why not?" With that, she grabbed Mathias' hand and joyfully walked beside him. Once again, she chattered on about seemingly nothing of interest to Mathias. Patty surely was a talker, the opposite of her present company (Mathias).

Stopping at his doorway, Mathias gestured for Patty to enter first, as he felt it would be a nice gesture. Patty smiled then walked into his room and Mathias followed behind her, apologizing for not having but one chair. He suggested they sit on the floor. Patty sat sideways in front of Mathias due to her having a dress on (so as to be lady-like). Patty spoke, saying she didn't like dresses. Yet her parents and the staff felt it would be proper while she was at Heilemann, being that she wouldn't be outside much anyway. Patty told Mathias she almost always wore long pants at home because she liked roaming around their estate where she lived. Looking intensely at Mathias, she asked him about his home life. With his face turned downward, he quietly said, "I really don't like talking about home." Patty instinctively understood why Mathias was closed in about discussing his home life. She felt a pang in her heart when Mathias looked downward. She said, "That's okay, Mathias. We don't need to speak of home." Gently, Patty reached over and laid her hand on top of Mathias' in a way of comforting him.

The two were talking and laughing at a joke Patty shared, both looking toward the doorway. There looking at them, was Ms. Strong clearing her throat. She spoke to Patty and reminded her young ladies weren't to be in a young man's room without an adult. Patty and

Mathias stood to face Mrs. Strong, and both said at the same time they were visiting before movie time. Mrs. Strong reached her right hand out to Patty and said, "Come along, young lady. You'll see one another at movie time and you two can sit together if you would like." They both smiled at one another and said, "Yes".

Mathias was left to himself until time to go the movie room. This gave him time to sort out some feelings he was having. Happiness was one of them. While in deep thought, he felt as though someone was watching him from the hallway. When he looked toward the door, he saw a wisp of mist flowing out into the hall. Then there was nothing but the doorway and quietness. Soon the loudspeaker came alive, letting everyone know that the movie time would be in approximately fifteen minutes. The voice stated for any, and all interested to start toward the movie room so they could possibly get a good seat. "Hurry along now," the voice said.

Entering the movie room, Mathias looked around. He spotted Patty waving to him to join her. She had her one hand on the seat to her left to alert others it was spoken for. She was also talking with another young girl to her right. As soon as Mathias made his way through the rows of seats to Patty, she turned her full attention to him. Greeting him with a smile and waving her hand to the seat next to her. Letting Mathias know the seat was for him. As soon as Mathias sat down, Patty seemed to glow with her radiant smile. Mathias turned toward her, and she quickly gave him a peck of a kiss on his lips. Then she giggled and so did her friend.

As the movie began, the lights were turned out. Only a dim light in the front of the room shone. The move title was One Flew Over the Cuckoo's Nest, starring Jack Nicholson. While Mathias sat quietly (paying total attention), he felt a hand fold into his soft and warm. He at first, didn't know how to react to the warm touch of Patty's hand touching his. His heart felt as almost an ache. Patty squeezed his hand as he looked over at her. He had a sheepish grin on his face. And he could feel the heat in his face.

Mathias knew not what to do. He sat very still trying to keep his focus on the movie while Patty kept whispering in his ear, just chattering away. Finally, Mathias motioned Patty with his left hand toward him where she could hear him. She leaned over to him; then he whispered to her, he really would like to hear the movie. She smiled and said, "Okay, Mathias." Still holding his hand, she sat quiet feeling at ease in Mathias' company.

Soon there was an intermission, which meant there could be soft drinks, snacks, and bathroom visits. Young men and young women made their way to separate sides of the room, to the bathrooms and the tables set up with drinks and snacks. Mathias made his way to a bathroom, waiting his turn. Then he went to a table where he picked a Coca-Cola and a blueberry flavored muffin while Patty chatted with her friend that sat with them sipping a Root Beer soda. A sudden movement caught Mathias' attention. There, (only faintly noticeable) stood Mr.

Granger in a corner, watching the milling around of all the people gathered in the movie room. Patty saw Mathias looking toward the corner where Mathias' eyes were directed.

She looked at the corner. There stood Mr. Granger. She recognized him, remembering the picture she had seen of him. Suddenly, Mr. Granger seemed to disappear in a ghostly mist.

Mathias then, was sure Mr. Granger wasn't among the living. Patty walked to where Mathias stood and asked, "Mr. Granger is not with us, huh?" Mathias felt another energy. He sensed his guardian close. He then walked away from the others. Walking toward the energy, he wasn't aware Patty followed him out of the movie room into the hallway, straight to where his guardian stood.   The guardian pointed past Mathias when Mathias reached him, speaking; letting Mathias know there was someone that had followed him. Then spoke, saying, "The girl, Patty, is behind you. You do need to be aware of your surroundings." Turning, Mathias stopped Patty before she took another step. Before he could speak, Patty asked, "Who is your friend, Mathias? Yes, I can see him." The guardian spoke to Patty saying, "Young woman, the young warrior needs to speak to me alone. Run along. Mathias will come to you when we finish here."

When Mathias returned to the movie room, the movie had already began. He found Patty in the same seat and sat next to her. While entering into the movie room, Mathias spotted Mr. Hammerman and Ms. Strong holding hands and her leaning into his ear. For they were seated into one of the darkest corners of the room.   Mathias was not accustomed to outward shows of affection. Patty slipped her arm into his which caused him to pull away a bit. Patty whispered in his ear, "It's okay Mathias. I just want you to know, I really like you." So, Mathias relaxed, still unsure of the feeling he was experiencing.

CHAPTER XI

Through the day, after Mathias and Patty were introduced, they seemed inseparable. For everywhere Mathias went (except the tests performed), there was Patty walking alongside him. The spiritual therapist asked Mathias, what was his take on the girl that stayed so close to him. Thinking on it, Mathias simply stated they had become friends; ones that understood one another. So, the days clicked by, which was filled with tests, a few movies, and the mysteries of the unexplained happenings. Also, Mathias was allowed on the grounds but never at night. Mathias and Patty together would gaze out the rear door window and discuss the stars. The owls would appear and voice their messages to the two of them. Once, a young doe sidled up to the door looking forlorn at the two of them, making small sounds (as if saying to them it understood their feelings of loneliness).

As Mathias knew and understood nothing is forever here on the earth, so he knew his time here would come to a close. He would be sent back to the ones (that acted around others) as they cared for him and his siblings. Mathias knowing within himself, changes were coming. He surely was not feeling good about returning to those two people. Yet he missed his siblings, especially Bethany. She always made his heart feel (what he could only describe as) love.

One night as he wandered down the hall, Mr. Granger came to him. Standing at arms' length, whispering to Mathias, "I am a victim of murder, Mathias." He then disappeared, leaving Mathias in a state of wonder. Reaching the rear door, he could see it wasn't completely closed. Pushing on the door, there was no sound as before alerting others there was a breach in security. Mathias felt a sense of urgency flowing through him walking to the right after he walked through the doorway. Seeing his way by the moonlight. Thinking it is journey time. Walking to a bush, Mathias hid himself behind it. For he heard footsteps. Knowing it could only be Patty coming to find him. Yet, it wasn't. He saw a longer figure than Patty holding something in their right-hand lurking around. Then the figure stopped and faced in Mathias' direction.

Suddenly, there was a loud shriek piercing the air. Then the voice screamed loudly, "Mathias! Look out!" With that, the figure ran toward the tree lines to disappear among the trees and bushes. Looking toward the scream, Mathias could make out Patty standing in the moonlight shaking. Mathias exited the bush rushing to her, grabbing her, and heading quickly to the rear entrance, to be met by Mr. Hammerman and Ms. Strong hurrying them inside.

Once inside, the two adults started questioning the youngsters of what happened. For they were walking the hallways upon hearing the loud shriek and Patty screaming Mathias' name, hurried to find the rear entrance ajar, and the two youngsters outside with Patty shaking, and Mathias rushing to her side. Mr. Hammerman guided Ms. Strong, Patty, and Mathias to the conference room. Once there, Mathias was asked how he was able to exit the rear entrance. Mathias explained that the door was slightly open when he reached it. He was going to explore the grounds more. Ms. Strong questioned Patty of why she screamed. Looking at Mathias, (Patty understood the blank look on Mathias' face) answering Mrs. Strong, saying she was frightened by Mathias Jumping from a bush and scaring her in jest.

Apparently, the two adults did not see the figure which ran into the trees. And Mathias wasn't telling them, nor was Patty. It would be kept between them. Then too, perhaps be spoken of later. Mr. Hammerman and Ms. Strong suggested the two children go to their rooms if they were calm enough to rest. Mathias agreed that the two of them (him and Patty) exit the conference room to retire to their own rooms. Thinking he would be able to meditate easily, the two youngsters went their separate ways.

While lying in his bed, Mathias lay in a comfortable position. For he had changed clothes and was wearing loose pajamas the facility had given him after his arrival there. Drifting in slumber, Mathias' mind could see figures of people, yet could not identify their faces. Suddenly he could see the room he was in fill with fog; like waifs drifting around, coming close to him, then turn away, one after another. Finally, one of the waifs came close to his face, yet was far enough away that Mathias could hear its voice. Waifs usually only make barely audible sounds (like little squeaks). Yet, this one voiced verbally enough so Mathias could understand. The message he received from the waif was to be kept to himself for all time.

The room cleared, leaving Mathias laying very still. Yet in a state of sleep where he could make out a sound of someone calling his name. Like far away, the voice became more clear saying, "Your brother, Grayson was found laying across one of the rails of a train track. Someone had drugged him and laid him there. It seems he is unharmed." The voice faded. Mathias then awakened from his meditation slumber. Sweating, trying to clear his mind of what he just heard. Knowing he would hear of it some time in the future. Instinctively, he knew who the two were that committed the act of laying Grayson upon the tracks. He also knew Anias would not believe him should he tell her. The only thing Mathias could do was wait for the incident to occur.

While waking, there came music over the loudspeaker. Music Mathias had heard on the TV at home and on a radio. Usually, he had heard only country music at home. That was mostly what Anias and Baxter listened to. So, he was accustomed to the sound. Country music for Mathias was moving. Yet not like Rock and Roll as it was called, and another music from black folks, known as Motown. Rock and Roll, along with Motown touched deep within Mathias. He realized he could dance to their tunes (a soulful sound indeed). This started the days of Mathias' awakening inside to music. He could move his body as well as he could to drums which stirred his heart.

Arising more from sleep, Mathias realized the music he was hearing was of a Motown artist he had already heard. He reacted by slowly moving his body to the rhythm of the music playing. Through the music, a voice spoke of a dance in the auditorium for all of the occupants at the facility. A time was designated for the occasion, "Earlier in the evening for 6:00pm", the voice said, "Be there or be square!" Mathias found that to be a funny statement. Mathias thought since the dance would be that very evening, he would practice dancing as long as the music remained playing on the loudspeaker.

While dancing to one of the Motown tunes, Mathias heard a knock on his door frame. Turning around to face the door stood Ms. Strong and a young lady. Mathias immediately stopped dancing. He felt embarrassed and it must have shown. For Ms. Strong told Mathias, "There is no need to be embarrassed Mathias. For you seem to know dance moves." The young lady with Ms. Strong quietly clapped her hands and shook her head in agreement. Smiling broadly, Ms. Strong asked Mathias, "May we enter, Mathias?" He nodded his head in a yes gesture (his face red). Then he stood there looking at the floor thinking, *'I must really look silly dancing alone, and not knowing how to dance'*. Ms. Strong sensed the boy's uneasiness and unsureness. She said to him, "Mathias, I brought Janie here to see if she could perhaps teach you how to dance. But apparently, you already know how." Janie walked to where Mathias stood and extended her right hand in a manner to shake Mathias' hand, saying, "I am Janie Wright, the dance instructor here at Heilemann". Mathias in kind, extended his hand to shake hands and said, "I am Mathias." The two women retreated from Mathias' room discussing the evening event, waiving to him as they exited.

Meanwhile, after the ladies' visit, Mathias just lounged around daydreaming; letting his mind relax. Relaxing, Mathias was interrupted with a knock. Opening his eyes to see Jenny Most standing there. She gave him a brief moment to gather himself. Then told Mathias she needed him to accompany her to the front office due to him having a phone call. The call, it turned out, was instead a note taken of the call by Mrs. Hopson. Entering into the office, Mathias could see by the facial expression on Mrs. Hopsons' face, that the news was not good. The lady offered Mathias a chair should he want to sit while she relayed the message in the middle of the room. Mathias spoke, saying, "I know what the note says. My sisters have been removed from the home by the Department of Family Services by order of a judge." Mrs. Hopson asked Mathias, "How do you know this?" Mathias looked at her and said, "I just know. They also want me to come home. I am not ready to go though. I want to finish here if that is possible." After a few minutes, Mrs. Hopson assured Mathias he would finish here at Heileman. She gave her word on it. She would handle the details. With that,

Mathias walked out of the office and headed toward his room, where he could find solace, at least for a short time.

Patty began preparing for the evenings' festivities choosing her finest dress (shin length), also choosing black shoes with double front straps and low heels for easy movement. She wanted to look her very best to impress Mathias, for she very much liked him. Mathias, on the other hand, was fretting due to his clothing. Ms. Strong came to his rescue, showing up in his doorway again (holding a cloth bag) smiling. Knocking, Ms. Strong walked in, handing the bag to Mathias. Also handing him a black pair of lace-up shoes which she called Bannisters. Mathias could only stand silently. Looking stunned, him asking, "Are these clothes and shoes for me, Ms. Strong?" She stated, "Mathias, these are for you. The staff pitched in for these things so you will be smartly dressed for this dance. And there is a young lady whom will be enjoying the evening of dance and fun with you." So, Mathias was set. He never expected anything such as he was experiencing.

Evening settling in, which darkened the hallways until the lights switched on automatically, lighting the way for the staff and clients. Mathias slowly dressed for the evening in the clothing the staff had procured for him (checking himself in the mirror all the while). His mind wandered around as usual. Him hearing, it seems most every noise that was audible. His thoughts were interrupted by a sharp voice scolding someone. Anias' face appeared before him, menacingly. Angry words spit out in a barrage of curses, as was her way. Mathias knew right that minute, her and Baxter were drinking and arguing over some little something that did not seem important to Mathias. Oh yes, it is the weekend he realized. The fight was on.

Mathias sat down in the chair in his room, reeling from the

vision in his mind. He sat quietly alone for that brief moment, so as to calm his mind and shut off the chaos going through him. A rap at the door brought him the rest of the way out of the vision. "Hello," said the girl standing in the doorway. "I see you are almost ready except your shoes and socks, Mathias." Looking toward the door, he sat upright. There stood Patty, grinning from ear to ear. What a beautiful sight she was. He wanted to whistle yet the sound wouldn't come out. For his mouth was very dry. So he just stared at her thinking, *'You are beautiful.'* Patty spoke, saying, "Come Mathias. We must be ready. The evening is to begin. And we can dance, and the time we'll have…" Mathias just nodded his head yes, then started putting on his socks and shoes. Patty walked to the little dresser and retrieved a comb. Walking to Mathias, she stated he should comb his hair. Looking up from tying his second shoe he said, "Okay Patty. Thank you."

Chapter XII

As Mathias and Patty walked to the dance, Patty linked her arm into Mathias' right arm (smiling at him). Once again, Mathias knew not what to say. So, he just smiled back at her with a sheepish grin. While walking, they both looked at each other strangely; wondering what that strange smell was coming from a room off the short hall they were passing. Stopping abruptly, Mathias cocked his head in the direction of the smell. Then quietly whispered to Patty, "How about we check out this strange smell before we go to the dance? I think we really need to do this." Quietly, the two of them made their way to the slightly open door. Peering inside, they observed Ms. Strong and Mr. Hammerman leaning over a table with their backs to the door. Mathias could see what they were doing. They were holding a rolled money bill while putting it to their nose and sniffing something white on the table. Passing the rolled bill back and forth and also something that looked like a rolled cigarette and snickering all the while. Mathias heard Mr. Hammerman say to Ms. Strong, "Let's finish here. We need to get to the dance, and no one will ever know our secret." Quickly, Patty and Mathias lightly walked to the hall they had previously been in, making their way down the hallway toward the dance. Mathias wondering what it was they were sniffing and smoking. Patty spoke, saying (as if she read Mathias' mind), "That was cocaine they were sniffing, and the smell was Marijuana they were smoking." Mathias asked Patty, "How do you know this?" She told him, from her mom and dad's friends. She observed them in the past doing both. Standing in the hallway was Mr. Granger pointing toward the direction they had just come from. Then he disappeared as if he were never there. Patty saw Mr. Granger also. Yet she told Mathias, "Let's just go and enjoy yourselves." Mathias answered, saying, "Okay."

Mathias and Patty entered into the auditorium where the party was just beginning. There was finger food, soft drinks, tea, and colorful reds, greens, white, and blues in the form of confetti. Someone had fashioned a banner of white with red lettering inviting all to enjoy the festivities. Walking through the cluster of people was Ms. Strong and Mr. Hammerman, whom had entered after Mathias and Patty. Smiling and laughing with others, they strolled across the floor. To Mathias, they seemed out of place with how they both looked, appearing to be nervous with slight jerky movements. No one else apparently noticed except Mathias, and perhaps Patty. Patty once again, laced her arm into Mathias' (lightly guiding him to a table the perfect size for the two of them). The room was beginning to fill with guests. Bringing with it a happy aura as the chatter grew with every passing moment. Mathias had brought with him small cotton balls to place into his ears so he could lessen the noise of all the chatter from so many talking, which grew louder and louder by the moment.

At the one end was a DJ set-up for the music, a man was plugging up speakers, the loud systems to produce the music, and a small stage had been built for the occasion to support the entire system. Which was not very large yet accommodating. There were cone-shaped napkins placed on the tables. And when stood up, alerted others the table was occupied. Also, nice tablecloths made of paper, shaped on the edges to reflect a classy touch.

Patty set the napkin so as to let others know the table was

occupied so her and Mathias could get themselves something cold to drink, and perhaps a few sandwiches, and a small variety of cut vegetables with different dips. She was very thoughtful of what she picked for them. Mathias stood and watched her at a short distance. Patty looked up and smiled an understanding smile toward him. After collecting what she figured they might want, Patty nodded to Mathias to follow her. Mathias sipping a Root Beer soda, shuffled in the direction Patty walked to bring them back to their table. With an ink pen, Patty wrote upon the napkin their names 'Mathias and Patty' adding a small heart.

Mathias sat thinking of what he and Patty had seen in the room where the two adults were engaging in smoking the pungent weed and the powder Patty had described as cocaine. This was Mathias first time seeing these things. He was curious about them. Little did Mathias know; it would be a detriment to his life. Now he must focus on the dance and music, along with the dance steps he had learned. He would find that his body moved to the exact sounds. Patty interrupted his thoughts by tapping his shoulder and repeatedly saying, "Mathias." Looking dumfounded, Mathias sheepishly replied, "Yes?" She attracted his attention by letting him know the music was about to start. Patty asked him, "Mathias, where were you? You apparently was deep in thought." Mathias answered, he was thinking on the scene they came across earlier on. On that, Patty cautiously told him to think no more on that and concentrate on her and the fun they would have. With that, Patty leaned over and landed a moist kiss on Mathias' lips causing him to blush red due to the kiss coming unexpected. The kiss was enough to redirect Mathias' mind and surely brought the boy to his senses. The recollection of Mr. Hammerman and Ms. Strong's doings would definitely come back to Mathias' young mind.

There was much chatter coursing around the room while waiting for the music to start. Meanwhile, the two youngsters (Mathias and Patty) sat enjoying the snacks, the soft drinks, their friends, and each other. Mathias excused himself for a bathroom break, caressing Patty's hair as he passed her. A male and female restroom sign, he spotted along a small hallway inset in one corner of the large room. Entering the hallway, a mist engulfed Mathias. Within the mist stood his guardian with a hand extended, inviting him to come see where his future may lie should he take the path he observed of the two adults this very evening. Mathias and his guardian floated along with the mist. Peering into the future years where his darkened journey would begin within another year. Mathias' mind began to reel from viewing the future events. Yet, seeing he would barely survive some of the most tragic times of his life. The boy (Mathias) entreated his guardian to take him back where they started. With that, Mathias found himself in the hallway once again where they met.

Patty came to find out why Mathias was gone from their table for the space of time he was absent going to the restroom. The DJ had started the music with a slow rhythmic tune. Motown for sure (The Platters) was in the air. So, Patty grabbed Mathias' left hand and hurried him to the dance floor so they could hug and slowly sway with the sound. The evening was filled with mellow music, nothing radical or outlandish. This Mathias liked. For the tunes reached his heart. He easily flowed to the songs. There was not shrillness in the music or surroundings. The chatter continued after each song, as did the soft drinks, hand holding between Patty and Mathias, also with a few others. Mr. Hammerman and Ms. Strong would sneakily leave the dance, as they were in a dark corner where there was a door leading into the main hallway (them, thinking no one would notice). Yet, they apparently paid little to no attention to Mathias. All the while he (Mathias) caught them exiting from his peripheral vision. Mathias grinned within himself, knowing he was probably the only one who did. As the boy (Mathias) understood, the smallest details can go unnoticed.

The evening was moving along with the soothing graceful body swaying tunes. All the time, Patty kept Mathias in motion with dances, talking, and occasional kisses. Yet, she too noticed Ms. Strong and Mr. Hammerman's comings and goings. The DJ was announcing a short dance contest for the ones that wanted to participate. He asked that everyone clear the dance floor so the contest could begin.

Patty grabbed Mathias' left hand, while insisting he lead her to the dance floor so that he would be a confident lead in dancing. Also, it would be a gentleman's way. A slow song started the contest with a few of the staff as judges on the dance floor, to observe closeup. Mathias and Patty holding hands on their one side of their bodies, while the other side their hands positioned thusly. Mathias' right hand around Patty's waist and Patty's left hand slightly around Mathias' right shoulder made for an excellent dance maneuver, where they could feel one another's' graceful moves. The staff moved around among the dancers in a way that would not hinder the young participants. There were six couples engaged in the dance contest. All seemed capable of moving with the music. Suddenly, the music changed to a quicker melodic beat, which the couples disengaged from each other to dance in a fashion to meet the changes in pace. Mathias and Patty took on a tempo that complimented both with movements unknown to the staff, yet the two were in sync. Others around Mathias and Patty moved away from them, so as to allow the two room for their moves.

The music tempo changed again to a slow beat, where the couples melded together smoothly (some awkwardly). The staff pointing toward 2 couples to exit the dance floor, eliminating them. To the amazement of the staff and others, the remaining four couples dance on. The music stopped; it was time for a ten-minute break. Patty once again placed her hand on Mathias'. And this time led him from the dance floor back to their table. She asked him, would he please get them a soft drink and a snack. With a smile, he agreed. Then hurried to the tables filled with snacks and drinks. While walking toward the tables, he was met by Ms. Strong. She stopped him to compliment he and Patty on their dance performance.

Ms. Strong inquired of their dancing ability. Mathias answered briefly that they felt each other's moves with the music, which enhanced the graceful movements for them. Mr. Hammerman made a slight movement toward Ms. Strong, letting her know to come his way. While at the snack table, Mathias watched them from the corners of his eye to see the two adults conversing quietly in whispers.

Mr. Hammerman along with Ms. Strong, strolled toward the side door. Thinking they were unnoticed along the way; Mr. Hammerman held his right hand to his side flexing three fingers in the direction of another couple. Presently, the couple made their way to the side door, thinking no one would notice. Mathias carefully watched the couples exiting the dance. He was wondering, *'What was the enjoyment of what they were doing?'* Within a few years, he too would be experimenting in those areas of drugs. The dance contest continued with elimination of another couple. Then came another break. Rest assured, Patty and Mathias were still in the contest. The two sat at their table, drinking their soft drinks, and munching on snacks.

Soon the four adults returned, claiming they were overlooking the hallways. Stating they needed the four of them to quickly finish their objective.

The dance contest resumed once again. Shortly, another young couple was eliminated; leaving Patty and Mathias, and another couple to finish the contest. The DJ announced there were but two couples left to compete for a prize. Excitement mounted. Suddenly all went blank for Mathias. He seemed to be drifting along in a void.

Mathias awoke with a startled look through dim glassy eyes, hearing voices unfamiliar to him. Mathias felt a hand on his left arm. Peering up, he saw a woman with tears in her eyes. She spoke, saying, "Son, I have prayed for you every day, hoping you would return to us." The woman disappeared before his eyes. Presently, another woman whom looked like a nurse, looked down at him. Seeing he had awakened, rushed out of the room calling for a doctor to come quickly.

By the time a doctor entered the room, Mathias was trying his best to sit upright. Yet, due to the weakness, he was not able to sit. Mathias' mind was foggy as if in a dream. A rush of air sounded, and he was back in the dance room; lying on the floor, with Patty and others looking down at him. Mr. Hammerman, along with Ms. Strong asked Mathias what had happened to cause his fall. They were helping him up and looking him over for any injuries he may have sustained; only to find a small knot on the right side of his head. Patty was almost in tears while the two adults sat Mathias back in his chair. "The boy had passed out due to overheating," Mr. Hammerman declared. "He will be fine." By this time, Mathias' mind was becoming clear. Mr. Hammerman asked him if he would be able to finish the dance. Mathias looked around him and saw everyone watching him. He answered yes, he could finish if the last dances were slow. Mr. Hammerman assured him it certainly would be.

Patty clasped Mathias' hand and assured him it would be okay, should he not want to finish the dance. Mathias felt he could. So, the two of them walked out to the main floor to continue. Many applauded Mathias and Patty as the two returned to conclude the dance contest. A slow tune began as the two couples swayed gracefully to the soft mellow music. Lights filtered around them in unison to the movement of the dancers. As the music stopped, Mathias looked at the DJ and sent him a thumbs up to make him aware that a faster tune would be fine. Smiling at Patty, Mathias said, "Let's give it our all to finish the contest." Patty readily agreed. The selected tune was not real fast. The two couples finishing the contest danced to another applause. During this dance, neither couple was eliminated all the way to the ending of the song.

The DJ announced the contest had ended. Also, the two remaining couples were tired. So, the prize would be awarded to the four contestants, which led to loud cheering, along with whistling and loud applause with a standing ovation. Confetti came falling on the contestants. Then came the shaking of hands all around. Mathias had placed cotton in his ears, so the whistles, yells, and applause wasn't bothersome to him. He and Patty were hugging happily when Mr. Hammerman, along with Ms. Strong and others came to congratulate the two couples. An announcement came, calling the couples to the DJ booth to receive their prize. When the applause subsided, the DJ announced the two couples, Mathias, Patty, Shelby, and Brian's names; saying the four contestants would receive the evening's prize. The couples would be dining at a nice restaurant in town along with their chaperones, Mr. Hammerman and Ms. Strong this very evening. The DJ suggested the two couples depart with the two adults so they would be rested and ready by 9:00pm. A cheer arose as the six left the dance floor.

At the moment, the time was reaching 7:30pm. The winning couples along with their chaperones would be leaving shortly for the restaurant to enjoy dinner. While waiting Mathias and Patty conversed looking out of the glass in the rear entrance of Heilemann. Presently, they observed a figure at the edge of the tree line, which seemed to be waiting on something or somebody. The figure started pointing in their direction. Looking at the figure, the two young ones (Mathias and Patty) were finally able to make out whom it was. To their surprise, it was Mr. Granger. Within a flash, he was gone as mist settled over the landscape obscuring anything in sight. Fog settled into a point the visibility was only a few feet. Mathias looked at Patty, saying, "There goes our dinner tonight." Presently, the both of them heard footsteps. Turning toward the sound, there was Mr. Hammerman with an apologetic look on his face. Standing still, the two children waited for the news Mr. Hammerman was about to give them, yet they already knew. The news of the fog that had suddenly forced Mr. Hammerman quietly told them the dinner engagement was off the for the evening. Yet another one would be scheduled shortly. The fog would only last for the night and early morning. The fog would dissipate by noon time. Mr. Hammerman had already informed the other young couple of the news.

The evening found Mathias and Patty sharing a meal in the dining hall, along with the other young people. There was much chatter amongst them of the evening contest. Others passed Mathias and Patty, congratulating them and the other winning couple. Grinning shyly, Mathias thanked the ones whom spoke to him and Patty. While eating, Mathias' mind wandered away from conversation with Patty to days gone by. Compared to now, the memories were worrisome for young Mathias. Empty spaces in memory seem to be a void in the life of such a young boy (Mathias). The memory of the State came into view. To Mathias, the scenery sounds, the pleasant and peaceful image of the store proprietors was a plus, and also the friendliness of the old dog brought a smile to Mathias. A patting on Mathias' arm brought him out of his reverie. Of course, it was Patty. She was asking him, "Where were you, Mathias?" All Mathias could do was to tell Patty what he was just daydreaming. Time seemed to stand still during the evening. Everyone was dispersing from the dining hall to head to their perspective rooms here at Heilemann facility. Mathias decided he would rest on his bed. There came a light knock on the door to his room. Jenny came to inform him his aunt was waiting on the phone to speak to him. Jenny assured him he wouldn't be going home just yet. She also told him he could tell his aunt the facility had not completed all the testing. He smiled a knowing smile. His aunt (Anias) asked him why they were taking so long. Mathias stated to Anias, "They hadn't completed the testing." In turn, she said to him, "I will talk to the head person of why the wait." Then she just hung the phone up with a slam. She never bothered to ask him how he was and didn't give him time to reveal the dance contest that he and Patty and the other couple had won. The two couples were very proud of their accomplished ability to overcome their young fears of so many people watching them perform their dances.

Mathias headed back to his assigned room. Standing in his doorway, was Mr. Hammerman, smiling. He extended his hand to the boy (Mathias) to personally congratulate him on his performance along with Patty being winners. The two (Mr. Hammerman and Mathias) stood silent for a brief moment. Then the man spoke quietly to Mathias, saying, "Young man, always be aware of where you walk in these halls. There are things you know nothing of." A rush of what sounded like wind came through the hallway where the two stood. Just as quickly, Mr. Granger stood between the two of them causing Mr. Hammerman to turn white from fear. Mathias grinning, asked Mr. Hammerman, "Had you seen a ghost, sir?" Mathias giggled as Mr. Hammerman exited the doorway and proceeded to run down the hall in the direction where Ms. Strong stood, dumbstruck, pale, and shaking. A ghostly laugh filled the hallway as Mr. Granger disappeared in a light mist.

Sitting alone, Patty taking in the night's event; the lights, the laughter, the music and the dance (partially wishing her and Mathias were older). She would miss him terribly, she knew. Patty was feeling a pain in her young heart. She would definitely talk to her friend, Lynda back where she lived. Lynda was a few years older than her. The girls would giggle while they talked as they always did. Only this time, a boy (Mathias) would be the subject of the talk along with Lynda's boyfriend (Grant). Patty had heard the rush of air and saw Mr. Hammerman and Ms. Strong walking quickly away from the hallway where Mathias' room was. She would ask him what had occurred even though she felt she knew some of what happened.

Mathias hadn't realized how long he had been at Heilemann. The time spent was enjoyable, yet he knew he would have to leave soon. For his aunt Anias was getting edgy since his sisters had been taken from of the home. Mathias decided he would speak to someone about their plans for finishing his tests and the results. Mathias lay on his bed, lounging in deep thought. He drifted in a half sleep, hearing what seemed a voice from the past saying, "Come and journey, Mathias. You know you want to." As he lay very still, another thought came through. *'Maybe I should run away from Anias and Baxter, back to my mother.'* Just as suddenly a thought came, *'Not yet'*. "There will be a right time." The voice that stated, (There will be a right time) he recognized, as the voice of his guardian. The hazy fog lifted from his mind. Mathias came out of the half-sleep to hear a light knocking at his doorway. Patty stood in the hallway, light seeming to also be in thought. Mathias spoke quietly, saying, "Patty, are you daydreaming?" Half smiling, she told Mathias, "I was just watching you sleeping. You seemed peaceful." The boy (Mathias) told her, "Come on in. We can sit in the floor and talk."

With that, the two of them sat in the middle of the floor. There seemed to be a light breeze, which caused the door to shut. They took it as a sign that they could be alone for a short time to talk privately. Neither of the two knew where to start. Mathias could see the pain in Patty's eyes, knowing they would part soon. So, they just sat in silence, looking into each other's eyes while tears rolled down their faces. Mathias was the first to speak. Understanding the moment, he took a deep breath, then spoke, saying, "The wind can carry away many things. Even though our tears sting over our faces today, we will remember all the moments we have here together. Let us let the wind carry our hearts through the years and remember the beauty of this minute in time." Patty, through broken words, told Mathias, "I will always remember you along with your laughter and the adventures we have had together. I will never forget you, Mathias. That is my promise to you today." All the while talking and crying, Patty and Mathias held hands. Mathias bent forward and kissed her hands, letting his tears fall on them and feeling no shame. Realizing he had not cried like this in the company of anyone that he had any memory of. So, young, the hearts. Perhaps he would be at the Heilemann a week or two longer. Patty spoke, asking him if he may be there a while longer. Mathias looked in her eyes and nodded a yes answer. It could be worked out to extend Mathias' stay, due to tests. That brought a weary grin to Patty's face, so her eyes shined through her tears.

CHAPTER XIV

Monday came as a bright sunny morning. Everyone gathered in the dining hall for breakfast. In, waltzed Ms. Strong; smiling like someone had let the cats out. Mathias and Patty sitting together, knowing what their grinning was about. The two adults sided up to the table where Mathias, Patty, and other couples were sitting together. Mr. Hammerman announced to the two young couples that their dinner reward would be this evening, suggesting they need to be ready around 8:00pm. Mathias stopped him in mid-sentence, relaying to Mr. Hammerman he (Mathias) and Patty would not be joining them for dinner. Mr. Hammerman started to insist, but Mathias quieted him with a wave of his right hand. Then telling him (Mr. Hammerman) it was done. They would have dinner here as usual along with the other clients. Ms. Strong stood stone still with a grim look, shaking her head. Mathias stood looking at the two adults and stated, "We know how hard everyone has worked to make the dance, the DJ, and the dinner arrangements. We appreciate all the efforts the staff have made. Yet, we have decided it's best we stay within the bounds of Heilemann. For we do not know what is in store for us. Being here, we know. He glanced at Mr. Hammerman and grinned. Mr. Hammerman answered Mathias, saying, "Sounds like you and Patty are sure of your decision. So, it will be so."

While Mr. Hammerman, along with Ms. Strong, and the other young winning dance couple made preparations for the dinner engagement, every one of the lunch occupants stayed in place. To enjoy the evening, the staff decided they would have a movie night in the dining hall since Mathias and Patty weren't going to dinner with the young couple and the two adult staff members. The staff had also secretly asked the cooks to make Mathias and Patty a congratulations cake and a special dinner (the staff's way of showing they cared and are proud of their accomplishment).

Suddenly came a clash of thunder which shook the windows of Heilemann. A lightning bolt split the largest tree in the rear of the property. Winds began to howl. Most all in the dining hall were affrighted, fear on their faces, except Mathias and Patty. The two looked at each other as they knew why the sudden burst of wind, lightning, and thunder shattered the evening. One of the staff rushed from the kitchen to try and calm the youngsters and other staff members; so as to keep everyone from running from the room. The wind, lightning, and thunder subsided as quickly as it started. A staff member walked to the side of the entrance to peer outside, seen not even a drop of rain had fallen, walked back to the center of the room, and announced, "It appears, it was a lightening flash with wind and thunder, now was over."

Everyone in the dining hall had quieted somewhat. Suddenly, on the loudspeaker, came a voice instructing everyone to quickly and orderly file to the building's secured basement. For a tornado was spotted twenty miles south of Heilemann, the voice warned. Patty and Mathias had already began to walk in the direction of where the voice had instructed with hurried steps; with others following behind, staff and all. As the heavy metal door was closed, staff was counting all the occupants to ensure everyone had made the exit to the basement, which was made for such emergencies. There were chairs, tables, blankets, pillows, food, and other essentials for the occupants.

Suddenly all could hear the destructive force of the tornado ripping apart stone, steel, and bricks of the facility. There were those that cried and prayed for their safety. Yet, Mathias and Patty remained calm. Setting against a wall holding hands, Mathias said to Patty, "It looks as though we'll be having to go home after this." Patty replied, "Yes Mathias. Surely, we will have to after this tornado is finished tearing this facility apart. There will be no record of our being here except in the memories of all of us." Mathias looked around the room; seeing most everyone sitting with their hands protecting their heads, with others sitting beneath desks, and those which could fit under chairs. The winds howled loudly, and the sound was like a freight train roaring. Off on one side stood his guardian calm, pointing to him, then coming near him and Patty. Speaking calmly, saying, "You are safe, young ones. Yet there is one that is perishing at this very moment. The children whom have gone are safe. The other adult has major injuries; will be taken to be cared for. Sit still and listen." Then the guardian disappeared.

Wind still blowing, yet not as loud. Rain pelted everything. It seemed the tornado was passing (hopefully subsiding), so as to do no more harm to the land animals and human beings. All had quieted from the tornado. A staff member breathed a sigh of relief, along with many others, to know the destructive force had passed. There were no windows in the basement shelter, which was a blessing in itself. All those that had their heads down and hands raised to cover them, slowly one by one, began to look up and see there was no one, or any objects, damaged in the shelter. A round of applause filled the basement to show their relief. A staff member spoke, saying, "Thank you, Lord Jesus, for keeping all here safe. And please watch over others that are outside of here. Thank you. Amen"

Many said, "Amen," also.

Now was the time for the staff members to try opening the large metal door so they could possibly assess the damage that was wrought by the F5 tornado. One each, of the male and female staff, walked to the door. Unlocking it and reaching for the metal handle pulled back on the door. It slowly opened causing debris to fall into the room. Holding the door, a staff member announced the entrance was blocked, yet they could see daylight. At the top of the debris is about a foot space. Water started to filter in yet wasn't a great amount that could cause flooding in the secured room. A staff member called for volunteers to help clear the doorway so they could possibly breach the outside. The two staff members could plainly see there was extensive damage to the facility, due to being able to see daylight.

Everyone crowded to the center of the large room to receive instructions on how to proceed in clearing the debris so someone could exit the room and come back in to give a report on the building and outside conditions. Instructions were given to form a line from the doorway to the farthest point in the room to pass debris through the line; to make space for whomever they decide to see outside for the task at hand. Everyone began lining up across the room so as to remove the obstacles blocking the door. Staff started pulling concrete and brick from the top of the debris and passing it to the next person, hand over hand, in a quick succession.

When the staff felt a space large enough had been opened from the pile of debris that occurred during the tornado in the doorway of the basement shelter, they talked of who would be willing to scale the pile and see how bad the damage was to the facility, along with the grounds. One of them stepped forward to volunteer, saying, "I will be the one to take on the task." Mathias, Patty, and the other young clients sat quietly during the discussion so the adults could go through the process of making a decision. Mathias quietly informed Patty there probably was not much left of the facility, beings' daylight could be seen when the big door was opened. In turn, Patty agreed with him. The head staff member was giving the man who volunteered instructions on what was needed to determine their next step to take. The volunteer went to the debris pile at the door and began to make his way upward toward the opening. While climbing, he could hear what sounded like a helicopter, whirring around above; hearing a voice from the copter on a loudspeaker, saying, "Someone is coming to help you." By the time the man climbing had reached the top, he was able to see outside and wave a hand so the one with the loudspeaker could see him. The voice on the speaker answered his wave, saying, "Help is on the way. They are bringing bull dozers and other heavy equipment to free all of you."

Once again, a cheer arose from the occupants of the basement. The man whom volunteered waved a hand to acknowledge he had heard. He climbed back down the debris and smiling, stated, "There is help coming to clear a path so we all can exit the basement." Quietly, he spoke to the other staff members; informing them the facility and the grounds were a total loss (trying not to alarm the younger occupants of course). Mathias and Patty's thoughts were confirmed.

While waiting, Mathias drifted into a half-sleep. Seeing home, he knew within he would be there soon. Especially with Heilemann being hit by the tornado, which totally destroyed it. Also, he visited with his guardian. During the visit, an angel of the lord appeared, speaking and encouraging Mathias to stay in prayer, as did his guardian. Abruptly, he was awakened by loud voices. The staff was speaking to someone outside, letting them know to direct everyone to the back of the room in three lines. Also, to cover their heads for protection in the event there was any debris falling in the room. For the rescuers would be starting within a few moments to clear the debris from the doorway of the basement.

Everyone in the basement scurried to the back of the room and line up as was suggested. Sitting in order, everyone covered their heads. One of the staff alerted the one outside that everyone was in position so they could start the debris removal. Everyone sat quietly listening to the machines' maneuvers with anticipation of being rescued. All sat thinking, as people will do, while hearing the rumble of the work to free them from their dilemma. Finally, all could hear the clearing of the door as they looked from their sitting positions. A little space in time, a man yelled inside, saying, "The doorway will be cleared within a few minutes. Then we can come in to retrieve you. Stay away from the door so you will be safe until we come in for you."

So, the rescue workers have made a way to clear the debris of destruction at Heilemann facility. They would soon free the staff and clients from the safety of the basement which was built to withstand the elements (such as storms and tornados), due to it being underground. Staff and clients alike began again to discuss the day's events; beings they would be free from their dilemma, making plans of returning home (which, some of the clients were not fond of the idea). Regardless of the clients' and even staffs' feelings, Heilemann wouldn't be there to serve them.

Mathias and Patty sat holding hands during the talk around them, (a bit tense and forlorn) knowing they may never meet again. Patty tried giving Mathias her family's phone number. Mathias refused to take it, saying to Patty, "My aunt and her husband would not allow him or his siblings to have access to the phone." While the two (Mathias and Patty) were talking, Patty moved closer to Mathias' side, therefore she was able to slip the phone number into his side jacket pocket without Mathias feeling what she had done, so she thought. Mathias grinned within himself, for he felt her hand feeling for his pocket. Yet did not act as though he knew.

By now, the rescuers and their machinery were at the door clearing away the debris while the onlookers in the basement watched silently. Staff and all stood in awe as the big doorway was being cleared and sighs of relief could be heard throughout the room, wondering how the outside would appear once they emerged from the heap of rubble. Mathias and Patty could not feel the excitement the others were experiencing. For today marked an ending concerning their future. Mathias felt the pang in his heart and chest, as did Patty. Both holding back tears, trying to accept what was inevitable for them. Patty smiled a wary smile toward Mathias, wondering would he be able to call her. For she knew he would want to. If only in her heart of hearts she knew for sure.

There came a loud clapping from the basement occupants, letting Mathias and Patty know they all would be able to leave the basement shortly. Patty grabbed Mathias and turned him toward her. She quickly wrapped her arms around him, tightly squeezing him almost breathless. She stepped into him as he wrapped his arms around her waist. They kissed a long lingering kiss. A farewell that can only be explained as a young lover's enchantment meant to be. Mathias told her he would call her as soon as their kiss had ended. Mathias stated, "I will find a way. It may take a while," yet he reassured her of it.

Soon, a staff member strolled over to them saying, "If you two can pry yourselves from each other, the rescuers have cleared the way so we can exit the basement." The two (Mathias and Patty) hesitated, holding on to their embrace for a few seconds more. Both with tears in their eyes, the two stepped back a foot from one another, hung their heads, and nodded an acknowledgement at the staff member. Making their way to the doorway, holding hands all the way to the door opening.

Sadness filled the hearts of most all the staff and those trusted with them when all saw the devastation the tornado had wrought as the occupants of the Heilemann basement walked out into the light. Murmurings could be heard as they straggled out to see what nature had bore upon the grounds of once was their respite; showing them all things here on earth are not permanent. Yet, God's beauty outside of the debris could also be seen far off. A thank you could also be heard. Mathias wandered off from the group, descending out of the basement. Patty followed after him to an untouched spot, where the ground hadn't been touched. The two (Mathias and Patty), taking in their surroundings. As they walked, Patty yelled to Mathias, "Hold on and I'll walk with you." Yet, he kept walking a distance, then stopped. Mathias could see his guardian and Mr. Granger, which seemed to be fading. The man vanished before their eyes. He was never to return. *'How sad'*, Mathias thought. He had grown fond of him. The guardian stayed at a distance, yet Mathias could hear him saying, "Take a good look, young warrior. It appears your life will take on the destructive path. You will look back many years later to see what you had come to be." Then, he too was gone. Yet not for good, as he had promised.

The staff informed everyone to stay within the group. And one of the staff walked to retrieve Mathias and Patty (to tell them to come to the group). For the buses was on the way to take them all to a safe shelter. There, the clients would have food, water, and a chance to shower before their parents, or whomever would come for them to take them home. Walking back to the group yet taking in what lay around them, Mathias, Patty, and the staff member whom retrieved the two children spoke not a word. A thunderous roar sounded in the distance. The group fearing the worst, praying silently that another tornado wouldn't appear. Mathias looked in the direction studying the clouds. He then stated to all, "It appears it is just a thunder cloud" heading in a direction away from them. Everyone in the group glanced toward Mathias. Then, set their sights on the thundering; grasping to acknowledge what Mathias already knew to not be a threat. Staff and children alike questioned in awe of how the young Mathias would know the thundering was of no danger.

Chapter XV

Five school buses began to arrive, brought comfort to all those waiting to be transported from the Heilemann destruction. A clapping of hands arose amid the sound of the buses and distant thunder. At least they would stay dry during the move. There were nothing to pack into the buses except themselves. So, the staff placed the children in separate rows so boarding onto each bus would be easier (naturally placing Mathias and Patty together so they would be comforted). Also paired the other children together with their closest companions for their comfort too; having staff members to pair off too (to act as chaperones) during the ride to a shelter an hour away from the destruction to ease everyone's anxiety.

Arriving at the motel, the motel owner met the group from Heilemann to welcome them with smiles from them and their staff. And to assure them preparations have been made for the large group's comfort. The owners stood to welcome the staff of Heilemann and the children. Speaking to the head staff member, informing her, their managers would be on duty for the group's stay. A young man named Jason, along with a young lady by the name of Mandy, strolled over to where the owner and the displaced group were gathering after the exit from the buses to greet them. During the conversation, the owner stated he must excuse himself and his wife, due to them having to travel to another one of their motels. Seems there were more people displaced due to the tornado. Saying their goodbyes, the man and his wife left the group in the care of the motel managers, waving as they left.

The two managers (Jason and Many) discussed the plans for the Heilemann group's stay. Jason spoke first, saying, "This is our plan to help your group be comfortable." Jason informed the Heilemann staff members the motel made arrangements for the boys to be on the upper floor and the girls on the bottom floor so as they would have their privacy. The staff would take the rooms closest to the office unless the staff would rather house with the children. It would be their choice. The Heilemann staff decided they would house with the children, as they felt the children would be more at ease with adults present. Mandy informed the group that there was food on the way from caterers in town. Her saying, "Okay everyone, let us begin by separating the boys in one group and the girls in another. Also, let us head to the rooms so everyone could shower and be comfortable while waiting on the caterers."

Mathias and Patty, along with a few other couples, straggled behind, hugging and assuring each other all would be okay. Patty held onto Mathias' hand with a grip that spoke of her deep emotional attachment to him. With the young emotions running deep, especially after a disaster that they had just experienced first-hand, her tears flowed as a stream down her face, wetting her lips. Mathias was saddened by her tears. Tears stinging his eyes, he swallowed hard to stop the flow. The moment came when the two had to part. Mathias, assuring her it would only be a short period before they would see one another this evening.

The boys scrambled to the upper floor, quickly choosing rooms; two boys to a room, beings the motel had many rooms which filled their needs. Showers were done hurriedly to accommodate the boys and staff. The staff members (while waiting for the children to refresh themselves) headed to the rooms close to the office so they would be available for the youngsters when they finished their showers. Mathias waited for the boy to shower. Then, he too, would clean himself up. While waiting, Mathias stepped out onto the upper walk for a few moments of lone time and quiet time where he could filter out all of the noise. Standing alone, Mathias could hear inside himself. He heard his oldest sister calling to him, calling his name, saying, "Mathias, come home." He could hear it as though she were close by. Inherently knowing at that moment, he would surely leave Anias and Baxter to go to his mother. When? He wasn't sure yet.

While listening, Chad (the other boy the staff had selected to be Mathias' roommate) called to him to inform him he could now shower, bringing Mathias out of his thoughts. Coming out of his reverie, Mathias could see a figure from the corner of his left eye standing at the end of the walkway near the stairs, a figure he did not recognize. He knew by the feeling, it was not his guardian. Stepping toward the door of his appointed room, he felt sadness. For the figures stood in a stooped position. He realized it was Mr. Hammerman. Mathias retreated to the room to shower, walking past Chad. Chad asked him, "Did you see the man stooped over by the stairway disappear?" Mathias nodded, acknowledging that the boy too could see spirits. Mathias went in the room to prepare for his shower.

When Mathias came back clean and dressed, his roommate informed him the caterers were setting the tables, loading them with fresh-made foods. The two boys nearly trotted down the stairway onto the parking lot toward the food loaded tables.

Awaiting Mathias was Patty beaming with anticipation of seeing him, with hands extended toward him. The caterers finished placing the food in order. They had prepared sandwiches of ham, chicken salad, along with roast beef, soups of different kinds, crackers, sodas, juices, and to top it off, desserts. Everyone started to sit down. A staff member stopped them, saying, "Let us all stand in prayer for our lives being spared and this beautiful bounty which has been laid before us." With that request, all present closed the gap between them to hold hands. Bowing their heads for prayer, the staff member started the prayer. The staff member spoke softly expressing gratitude, humbly asking for mercy for the Heilemann residents whom made it through the tornado, the people in the surrounding areas that was affected by the destruction, the creatures, the earth, and those lost to the tornado. As the prayer closed, one could hear sobbings of joy and sorrow. Patty being one of those emotionally affected; she clinged to Mathias' hand tightly. Also knowing they would part shortly.

The catered meal was a sight to see, being it was prepared by professional caterers, very mouthwatering. Everyone standing sat down to enjoy the meal laid before them which brought a rush of voices, due to the passing of different food plates. Mathias and Patty sat quietly, whispering during the talk and passing of plates containing food to be consumed. They both had taken of certain foods during the passing of plates. Mathias looked upward toward the sky due to seeing a large, winged shadow. Patty followed his gaze, also seeing the shadow, Owl passed overhead, coming almost within arms reach of the two. Patty inquired of Mathias why the bird come so close. While all those tables looked on, some with fright and some with wonderment, Mathias leaned over to Patty quietly saying, "The owl brought a message of the future, which I will learn later. Let us enjoy the meal."

Thunder spoke in the distance of an ominous storm, which appeared to move away from them, sparking lightning from a dark sky. Patty jumped at the loud clapping thunder. Mathias quieted her by holding her left hand. She smiled and winked at him.

The thunder spoke of hidden-unspoken secrets of the heart with the two young teenagers (Mathias and Patty), where both hoped one day would be possible (their hormones starting to surface). Mathias recognized the feelings he experienced, wondering if Patty felt the same. *'What a time,'* though Mathias, storms following enjoyable moments in his life. Peering off into the wooded area, Mathias felt the strong need to return home to wander the woods again despite the conditions there. He could sit silently among the forest and ponder on his longing to escape Anias and Baxter's drunken fights. He knew within, he would one day be out of their reach, not realizing the years to come walking in chaos his guardian had warned him of the coming years. The boy wondered how he would feel in these years. Patty tapped Mathias' shoulder, saying, "Mathias, you are daydreaming again. It seems to be your favorite pastime." She giggled afterward because Mathias jumped at her touch and voice. He looked at her and smiled saying, "Yes. I was daydreaming."

Patty, looking somber, told Mathias their time was getting shorter for them to be together and would he please not wander off in his mind. Also, to spend this time enjoying the happy times they've had and will have. Now for these few hours, as the group basked in the large selection of foods laid before them, there was much chatter of the months past and the sightings around Heilemann. One thing they all had in common in this entourage was the lingering feeling of closeness with one another considering all they had shared. Stories were recounted, laughter along with tears was expressed openly, a feeling of gaiety passed through and around them.

Mathias arose from his seat, coaxing Patty with him, walking the length of the table they occupied, to speak with the head of the staff. Reaching her and asking for permission to speak, the head lady acknowledged Mathias, saying, "Yes, you may." Mathias (clearing his throat) asked, "Ma'am, may Patty and I take one last stroll in the woods to be with nature in order to say our farewells to one another and the creatures that we encounter? Please?"

With that said, the staff member assured Mathias and Patty that surely would be fine, in saying she informed the young couple that the buses would be leaving, taking them to where their families would be waiting for them; so please listen for the horn.

So, off went Mathias and Patty, trodding along towards the wooded area where quietness awaited them. In the distance stood a long figure watching their movements as the two made their way into the forest that seemed to be untouched by the storms. Hiking hand in hand, the two young souls lanquished in the moments they would always remember sharing their lasting memories quietly. Mathias stopped and faced Patty searching for the words, knowing this was probably their last time they would see one another. His heart hurt with the knowing, yet he smiled his sheepish grin. Patty, seeing in his eyes what he couldn't bring himself to say. So, she spoke, saying, "Mathias, our hearts are young. There will be much in this life to face. The bond we have was given to us to relish for a lifetime." The tears fell down both their faces as a waterfall. They came together in a tight embrace shaking them to their core.

Suddenly, a branch broke. The two turned toward the sound. There before them, stood a black bear on its hind legs, just looking at them. Hearing a sound behind the bear, both youngsters peered past the bear. A tall figure that had been watching them came into view. Striding up to them and the bear was Mathias' guardian. Touching the shoulder of the bear, the guardian spoke in an ancient language to the creature. Mathias' guardian then spoke to Mathias, saying, "The spirit of the Black Bear would be with you throughout your life." Suddenly, the bear turned and made its way through the forest, leaving them standing with the guardian. Patty breathed a sigh of relief, but still shaking inside. The guardian smiled at the two young people. Then spoke, saying, "Many years will pass. Then you two will reunite in your older ages. Then there will be peace within you." Mathias understood the passage of time, yet not knowing the length of years to come. The young couple came together again as the guardian vanished as quickly as she had arrived. Mathias and Patty kissed a long lingering kiss with tears wetting their faces together. Then sounded, a long horn (their signal to return to the group). The time had come to part. They stood facing each other, holding their trembling hands in each other's, not wanting to let go of the moment. Yet, knowing they had to. Mathias spoke, "This will always be. Let us go and venture into our lives and treasure what we hold in one another. "Overhead, a hawk flew among the trees, sending its farewell sound loudly, echoing it's message.

Mathias and Patty wiped each other's tears and kissed one last time. Then came voices calling to them. Hand in hand, they started walking in the direction of the voices. They let their memories linger among the forest, echoing through the branches and along the valleys. The two would lock their minds for all time. Aho!

Chapter XVI

Walking back to the parking lot, Mathias and Patty felt the first drops of light rain singing softly. They could hear the comforting sound on the roofs of the hotel buildings and the pavilions. Watching all that were running to the pavilions for cover, while the young couple slowly stepped onto the parking lot (hearing the others calling their names trying to hurry them).

Patty and Mathias approaching the pavilion closest to them, Mathias could smell coffee, thinking to himself. Perhaps he would buy some. For he had never tasted coffee; the notion sounded right. The two strolled onto the pavilion and Mathias made his way to the coffee pot. Reaching for a cup, pouring it, smelling the aroma, feeling a sense of freedom to choose what he wanted in that moment of time. Mathias tipped the metal cup to taste the coffee. And wouldn't you know, a staff member approached him reaching their hand to retrieve the cup. Mathias stepped back speaking to the staff member, saying, "Excuse me. I am to drink this coffee and you will not interrupt or take it from me. That is final." In so doing, Mathias tasted his first drink of coffee in the presence of all. Letting the taste linger on his tongue, he liked it.

Then came the head staff member to inquire what the issue was before him. Seeing Mathias with the cup of coffee, he spoke, saying, "Now, Mathias, you know the coffee was prepared and given for the adult staff." Mathias in turn, spoke, "Yes sir, I know that. It smelled so good, and I wanted to feel that I had a free choice to experience the right and freedom of my choice. I wasn't being rude. I just wanted to be able to enjoy my first taste of coffee." The head staff member nodded a yes gesture, waived his hand in agreement, then informed the other staff member to let the young man be.

Buses sounded their engines in readiness of the journey the clients and staff were embarking on, ready to face the rain and fog that was developing around them. There were many goodbyes from the young and older riders. Staff, making a way for the clients also talking, where each staff member could do their best, according to the young peoples' needs. Therefore, staff members would occupy front seats of the buses and along the line of seats for convenience.

With the sound of the bus engines, all knowing they would be boarding for the ride toward their separate destinations. One of the young people blurted out with a guffaw of laughter, "All aboard. Let's do it." With that statement, many started making their way to the line of buses slowly. Staff members had gathered along the line of buses, so they were ready to receive everyone. With information on paper of each client, along with their information to assure everyone arrived approximately where their families could receive them.

Mathias, Patty, along with others in their circle, knew each of their newfound friends would not be riding together. For each of them lived in different counties across Missouri, including a few clients residing in a few other states. Those few young people would possibly be riding trains home.

Everyone saying farewell felt bittersweet amongst them all. For they spoke the words to one another. Boarding the buses began. Mathias and patty shuffled along at a snail's pace to be interrupted by a staff member telling them to move along. Patty's bus was the first in line. Mathias' was behind hers idling. The drivers were growing restless due to the waiting period, waiting for all to board.

Mathias and Patty holding hands tightly, savoring their last minutes in the realization they may never see one another ever again. With tears rolling down their faces, the young couple finally had to part ways. Hurt tearing at their young hearts, Patty took the first step on her assigned bus. Leaning to kiss Mathias goodbye, then whispering, "I love you, Mathias." They both looked to the sky upon hearing the sound of the Bald Eagle expressing a farewell from the area.

Walking away slowly (holding back the tears), Mathias straightened his shoulders holding his head high, made his way to his assigned bus, thinking, *'Don't look back.'* For had he, the tears would surely flow in and endless stream. In Mathias' ears, he could hear many voices. One sounding over all the others, Patty's resounding voice as an echo, then fast footsteps running toward him. Turning around, seeing Patty. She almost collided with him. Throwing her arms around Mathias (her face totally wet with tears), locking a kiss on him, holding him so tight, shaking uncontrollably. Mathias felt even her legs trembling. This brought the young boy to tears overflowing once again. Needless to say, the young couple's parting (Mathias and Patty) brought tears to many others, including some of the staff. Then came a loud shout of hooray from all and much clapping for their courage. What a farewell. The bus drivers started sounding the bus horns when the clapping and cheering began (an event that would not soon be forgotten).

Mathias and Patty's parting stayed with the both of them for years to come, now waving from their assigned buses. Waving until the buses parted in separate directions. The two young ones feeling their first heart break, yet first love; Mathias viewing the landscape slip away. This adventure would remain always in his heart as a treasure.

The sound of the bus motor and tires took Mathias into daydreaming a light sleep. While others conversed concerning their own memories of time spent at Heileman, including their adventures (which to them was an important part of their life). Mathias and Patty would have stories for their families. Yet, Mathias actually would have no one to share this part of his life with, except his oldest sister, Bethany.

Mathias riding along, listening to the whining of the bus tires, smiled to himself remembering his time at Heilemann; the days of clinical tests, his nights, and the dance off. Images, as dreams waltzing through the young man's mind (a tapestry: sharp, clear, and colorful). Leaving a seemingly pleasant feeling of knowing as euphoria.

A jolt brought Mathias out of his reverie. An accident ahead of the bus Mathias and other clients and staff were traveling on, stopped suddenly to avoid hitting the vehicle in front of them. Traffic was at a standstill. Sirens blaring pass the bus as an ambulance and police cars whizzed by. Everyone peering out the windows. Even a police car passed them on the shoulder of the road, headed for the accident. Someone on the bus spoke a prayer for those involved in the accident.

In approximately an hour, traffic began to move slowly signaling the occupants on the bus. Leaving some with a feeling of relief, yet some were weary of returning home. Mathias was one of them, feeling thusly. Now through the chatter, Mathias once again closed his eyes to slumber, listening to the sound of the tires humming on the asphalt. Him, feeling a peaceful energy come over him.

Miles passed as Mathias, along with a few others, slept leaving the care of worry or concern to those whom would worry.

For Mathias surely never worried. He felt it wasn't necessary. For he felt it would only leave a person gloomy and stressed.

Mathias awakened to the sound of someone talking loudly. Peering through half open eyes, he sees the bus driver and a staff member calling out names, alerting the clients that were to be met by family or friends. Their destinations had been reached. As Mathias watched others exit the bus, he knew his exiting the bus wouldn't be long now. So, he held on to the peaceful feeling inside him.

Sitting in a comfortable position, Mathias could contemplate on his thoughts of a certain subject that has overtaken many other thoughts, due to his journey at Heilemann which brought him with a measure of peace. He (Mathias) knew Mr. Blackwell would be at his drop- off spot. Then it would be a short ride to Anias and Baxter's house. Home; where living with them and his brothers continues.

Mathis was hashing a halfway plan. Yet being impulsive, his planning didn't consist of a lot of detail, and he would not be sharing it with anyone. Opening his eyes, Mathias recognized the town he had left behind. A small tinge of dread shot through his being. Then subsided as quickly as it surfaced. Mathias closed his eyes to relish the visions in his mind, of the feeling of peace while he was away from home. Sights and sounds filled his head. Seeing Patty and times they shared. Also, the others he had come to know. Much had changed with him. He felt the change strongly, realizing chemical changes also.

Shutting out the noisy chatter. He (Mathias) could hear it, yet he did not let it interfere in his reverie. Once again, the young boy cleared his thoughts to focus on the moment's journey.

For within a few moments, he would meet with Mr. Blackwell. Which would be the final transportation to where the family had recently taken up residency in Butler County, Missouri (Poplar Bluff).   Where Mathias could see as an improvement from where the family had lived on the mountain, the vegetation, along with the park in the lower valley. The animals all were missed by Mathias.

While peering through the bus windows, Mathias could see Mr. Blackwell standing, viewing his area (always watchful as he had been trained to). Mathias blinked, realizing this journey to Heilemann Institute, and his return to his living environment finally felt like a door slamming shut. It actually physically jolted him.

Exiting the bus, Mathias looked around curiously at what appeared to be changes in this town. He could see its growth in the somewhat short period the boy had been gone. Mr. Blackwell greeted Mathias with his right hand extended in a gesture of shaking hands. Which Mathias promptly put out his own right hand in response to Mr. Blackwell. Mathias could see the Tasty Freeze Drive Inn place to eat and have ice cream treats along with root beer floats and other like treats.

Mr. Blackwell started their conversation with a welcome home. Adding with it, him saying he was glad Mathias wasn't harmed due to the tornado. Mathias could only partially grin and say, "Thank you, Mr. Blackwell". The two (Mathias and Mr. Blackwell) strolled to the car which had an emblem on the two front doors. It read, 'Juvenile Officer'. This caught Mathias' attention. Seeing his reaction, Mr. Blackwell assured Mathias all would be well, and told Mathias he had taken the job to better serve the youth in the county; little did Mathias know.

Mathias partially understood life was on the verge of change for him. The young Mathias could only guess what and where. All was in the future, for sure. The ride to Anias and

Baxter's was the start of a new era in Mathias' life. Which would certainly not be much longer.   Again, with Mathias' impulsiveness, even he wasn't sure of how it would come about. Riding through town, the young boy was quite unsure of how the days would bring peace to his heart and mind, rehashing the violence around the house with Anias and Baxter. Mathias thought on how he would avoid the two adults as much as he wanted peace. One thought came. He would retreat into the forest to find calm. His sister Bethany was there now to search for him. He would ride the wave of chance and let it carry him away in his mind.

Should Anais or Baxter ask questions of his time at Heilemann, Mathias would wing it. He could sit silent as he has done since early age. He will deal with it.

Mr. Blackwell casually drove around the town, so as to ease Mathias' uneasiness that he recognized in the young boy. Knowing Mathias was not ready to be back with Anias and Baxter, the man hoping Mathias would be more at ease when the two of them (Mr. Blackwell and Mathis) finally arrived at their destination. Mathias half-heartedly, with a slight grin, asked Mr. Blackwell if he could just take him (Mathias) to the outskirts of town and leave him there, trying to sound as if he were joking. Mr. Blackwell looked at Mathias with a half-grin, saying, "I know nothing would please you more than to journey elsewhere. Yet, I have an obligation to fulfill with the family and the state. So, I must stick to it. Sorry, Mathias. This is what we have to do, is to get you to your foster aunt and uncle." That concluded the conversation.

Mr. Blackwell set the pace of the official vehicle in the direction of the residence he was instructed to deliver Matias to. The man (Mr. Blackwell) trying to explain to Mathias the obligations in life, so maybe the boy could understand his role in this life. Mathias politely listened, but his mind wandering elsewhere. Finally, Mr. Blackwell asked the boy if he understood. Mathias half-heartedly answered with a yes, he understood. The moment came when the two arrived at the driveway of Anias and Baxter's house. Gravel crunched beneath the vehicle's tires as if a signal to Mathias he was back in his unwanted environment. Hearing the German Shepherd dog (Rocky) barking also, as the two entered the long driveway leading to the house. As they came to view, there stood Anias, waiting seemingly impatient, fidgeting, with her hands and a cigarette, standing on the old wooden porch (a half wrap around style). Yes, they had moved them again. The former house burned completely. Mathias knew why. Everything he had, clothes and all, went up in flames once again. But had they?

Coming to a stop at the end of the gravel, an uneasiness settled into Mathias. His inner warning system working at full capacity, let the boy know to be aware at all times, especially with the nervousness of Anias.

Mr. Blackwell nudged Mathias, saying, "Well son, here you go. Try and do your best with that," he grins. Mathias could only wonder if it all, so much in him had changed. Especially the newly felt freedom of being out away from prying eyes, from these at home. Okay, the moment had arrived. No one here but Anias, Baxter at work, and the boys gone to school.

Anias seemed to bounce off the wooden porch, halfway running to the vehicle Mathias and Mr. Blackwell were starting to exit. Anias was now in front of Mathias (holding her arms out in a gesture of wanting to hug him). Mathias let her hug him. He, trying to avoid the cigarette Anias was holding. While Anias was hugging him and before exiting the official vehicle, Mathias' eyes were taking in the surroundings: woods, bushes, and animals scurrying for cover, a field mouse perhaps, a log with both ends open (wasn't but a distance of, maybe 100 feet away). A tall oak caught his eye. For setting in the top sat an owl, hooting a forlorn sound. Anias let go of Mathias and said, in a haughty voice, "Look Mathias, your friend has come to welcome you home." Mathias only half-grinned thinking, '*Owl came to warn me of things to come.*'

Anias, acting friendly, invited Mr. Blackwell in for coffee or something cold to drink. He accepted, saying, "I do have time for a refreshment. Then I can discuss some things concerning Mathias, Heilemann Facility, and its untimely destruction. Mathias asked if he could be excused so he could wander out into the woods to explore his new surroundings. Anias turned her attention to him, saying, "I would rather you wait until Mr. Blackwell leaves, after we have coffee and cold drinks, and talks are finished."

Mathias just stepped in line with them and let his mind wander back to Owl's message. He could decipher it, and to figure it out later. Walking forward the boy waved his right hand in a slice at waist height to inform the owl he would understand its message. Mr. Blackwell asked Mathias about the hand motion he just saw. Anias listening, spoke and informed Mr. Blackwell that Mathias seems to believe he has understanding of the creatures. Mathias again, just grinned.

Mathias sat quietly while Mr. Blackwell and Anias rattled on as Mathias took in sights and sounds. The talk seemed to linger on. Anias was curious of the events at Heilemann. Mr. Blackwell informed Anias that Mathias, Patty, and another young couple won the dance contest. Anias looked at Mathias and spoke, saying, "Mathias, you never told me of this."

Mathias, in turn, said, "I tried to tell you." Anias quickly changed the subject. Mr. Blackwell could see the tension. He (Mr. Blackwell) stood and excused himself, saying, "I must get back to my duties. I have a couple teenagers I must go and see about." With that, Anias (getting up from her chair) extended her hand to Mr. Blackwell to shake his hand in a friendly gesture. Then letting her hand linger in his, Mathias noticed her little finger scratching the palm of Mr. Blackwell's hand, ever so lightly. Later on, Mathias would understand the gesture. Mr. Blackwell knew what it entailed and promptly withdrew his hand, looking to see if Mathias was aware. Mathias had averted his eyes away so as not to be detected.

Mr. Blackwell turned and made his way to their front door. All the while rubbing his hands together. *'Sneaky people'*, thought Mathias. Anias wasn't aware of the hand rubbing. Her and Mathias made their way to the driveway to say farewell to Mr. Blackwell. By then, Owl had retreated.

Standing at the driveway Mathias knew at that moment, this day marked a new chapter in his life. Where it would take him he knew naught of what, when or how. But he knew.

Epilogue

As I set here today, I have reflected on events in my life. My siblings and I were partially raised in the hills of Southeast Missouri, during the time when many families were poor in the 1950's (not long after the great depression).

At this time in our lives, families hand picked cotton in the Southeast and also in Arkansas, mostly for a day's wage. Which amounted to nearly nothing, yet we survived. Bologna and bread was our lunch in those cotton fields. It was cheap back then, yet we had to work hard to get even that.

I look at now. What I see is people have changed and not for the good. Strife and grief come hand-in-hand. The Lord Jesus and our Father in heaven has told us in the Good Book (Bible) as some call it, this will be in our time. You do not have to believe me. Just read the word that Jehovah (God) sent down for us to read and understand.

I have not gotten off track. I feel this message was to be given to those that will read and understand. Also, to take heed to.

Now, back to Mathias. He is the reflection of me coming up through the years. His hardship and his joy has brought him through by the grace of God.

My oldest brother has passed on, as has our mother, a sister, a baby brother, and another younger brother. Also, one of my daughters has passed, Anastasia King.

What doesn't kill you makes you stronger, as is said through these books. You, the reader, will get a glimpse of life and its many struggles. There is also joy to feel.

Thank you, my readers. For hearing these words. For they are true. Also, there is fiction laced into Mathias' journey.

Thank you.

Sincerely,

Gordon Beck